RIVIERA LIAISONS

RIVIERA LIAISONS

Ian Fenton

Published by
Matador
12 Manor Walk, Coventry Road
Market Harborough
Leics LE16 9BP, UK
Tel: (+44) 1858 468828 / 469898
Fax: (+44) 1858 431649
Email: books@troubador.co.uk
Web: www.troubador.co.uk/matador

ISBN 1 899293 43 4

Typesetting: Troubador Publishing Ltd, Market Harborough, UK
Printed and bound in the United Kingdom by Henry Ling Limited, at the
Dorset Press, Dorchester, DT1 1HD

Matador is an imprint of Troubador Publishing

*To Helen for doing God's work so bravely
and always thinking of other people.*

Chapter One

Peter peered into the mirror and adjusted his tie. He concluded that it went well with his dark brown suit. He reached for his comb and gently eased his hair into shape, allowing it to fall partly over his forehead. He looked irresistible, he decided, or close to it as he smiled at his reflection in the mirror. He also felt a trifle nervous. In a few minutes he would be meeting Kay's best friend, Mandy, for the first time and he was anxious to make a good impression.

Kay had suggested the foursome when he had been talking to her husband, Jim, his best friend, at their house the previous week. She was charming, vivacious and attractive and Peter had always got on well with her ever since he had been Jim's best man at the couple's wedding three years before.

'I've got a close friend at work, Peter, I'd like you to meet her.'

Peter was caught unawares by her audacity, but he smiled at her nevertheless.

'Really, Kay. You're not trying to marry me off again, are you?'

'Don't be silly. I just thought you might like to meet her, she's a lovely girl, so unspoilt and genuine. Why don't the four of us have a drink together one evening?' said Kay, warming to her task.

'She's very pretty,' added Jim, grinning at Peter.

But it was Kay who was the architect of the fateful meeting. She was the inventive one who thought she saw the potential for a perfect partnership between two of her friends. Many months later, when Peter recalled her enthusiasm, he wondered if she would have recoiled in horror if she had foreseen the repercussions that would ensue from her well-intentioned matchmaking.

Peter glanced at his watch. They would be arriving any time now. He gave his brown slip-on shoes a quick rub with a duster and finished off his cup of coffee. The house was clean and the kitchen tidy so if they wanted to come in for coffee later he was well prepared. He heard a horn – that must be them. A final glance in the mirror and he

1

was ready. He grabbed his coat and keys and made for the front door.

On the way to Jim and Kay's favourite pub, The Rose and Crown, Peter sat in the back of Jim's Vauxhall Cavalier with Mandy. He found himself attracted to her immediately, as she seemed so nice and friendly.

'Do you like your job at the bank?' he asked her.

'Yes, I enjoy it, I like most of the people I work with. I've been there almost two years now. Kay and I usually manage to have the same time off for lunch and we quite often go to the pub around the corner.'

Peter liked her easy, open and natural way of speaking and his eyes appreciated her pretty looks and long blonde hair.

The large attractive olde-worlde pub was quiet, with only a few customers, as Peter bought the first round of drinks. He handed Mandy her half of lemonade shandy and sat down beside her. As the evening progressed he found himself more and more attracted to the charming girl with her bubbly personality and infectious smile. He was delighted to see she was not a heavy drinker. Peter hated that in a young woman! He had to coax her into having a second glass of shandy and when she was offered a cigarette by Jim she politely refused.

'Why don't you give up that disgusting habit?' Peter good-naturedly asked Jim.

'Easier said than done, old chap. I did manage to stop once but then I repented and started again.'

'Think of all the money you'd save,' added Mandy, taking Peter's side.

'Hey, you two are ganging up on me. Kay has never minded me smoking – have you, darling?'

'Whatever makes you happy, love, but I gave up years ago. I don't fancy dying of lung cancer.'

'This is a conspiracy. I don't care what any of you say, I'm definitely going to satisfy my craving and nobody is going to stop me,' replied Jim, reaching into his jacket pocket for his lighter.

'We don't mind if you want to kill yourself,' responded Mandy as all four of them dissolved into laughter.

'I think I care a little bit,' said Kay once the laughter had subsided, putting her arm inside her husband's. Jim responded by giving her an affectionate peck on the cheek and taking a long puff on his cigarette.

The conversation did not flag once throughout the evening and by the time they decided to leave Peter was convinced the night had been a great success.

As Jim drove to Mandy's house Peter had a few brief moments to reflect. He already knew he wanted to see her again. He liked the way she had intervened and supported him over Jim's smoking. He liked the way she listened and showed interest when he talked about his job as manager of an insurance agency in Torquay and his leisure activities at the local sports centre in Paignton. Should he ask her out tonight or should he wait a few days and then phone her? It was a difficult decision but he decided on the latter course of action.

'You live with your parents, do you?' asked Peter as they approached Mandy's house.

'Yes, Peter, and my younger brother, Bobby. He's nineteen and at university a lot of the time.' She disappeared into the house waving as she started to close the front door.

Now that they were alone in Peter's house, drinking a cup of coffee, Kay was eager to find out what Peter thought of her friend. He was not surprised as he knew she was never shy at coming forward.

'What do you think of her then?'

'She's a very nice girl, Kay,' responded Peter, 'as I would expect of any friend of yours.'

'Flattery will get you everywhere, dear boy,' said Kay, laughing.

'How old is she?'

'She's twenty-four,' replied Kay. 'Four years younger than you. Just the right age. Are you going to ask her out? I'm sure she'd like you to.'

'Leave the poor guy alone, darling, he's only just met Mandy,' interjected Jim.

'No, it's okay; I'd like to take her out. What's her telephone number?'

Peter saw a wide smile and a look of contentment light up her attractive face. Kay searched in her handbag for a piece of paper.

'She's a super girl, Peter,' said Kay. 'I'm sure the two of you will get on like a house on fire.' Peter smiled and offered her another plain biscuit.

Kay's reading of the situation turned out to one hundred per cent correct. Peter took Mandy to the multiplex cinema on Paignton seafront. They saw *Angela's Ashes*, which Mandy in particular enjoyed. Afterwards they had dinner in the plush restaurant. They lingered over the coffee and mints.

'It's the first time I've been in the restaurant, Peter, it's very nice.'

'Yeah, the cinema seems to be doing quite well. I think it was a good idea to turn the old theatre into a modern eight-screen cinema. Even the summer shows don't attract people like they used to and the big stars don't want to do three-month summer shows any more. Besides we've still got live shows at the Princess and Babbacombe theatres in Torquay and the Palace Avenue Theatre in Paignton.'

'Can we go for a walk along the seafront in a minute?' asked Mandy.

'If you want to. Have you finished your coffee?'

They walked hand in hand, past the pier, to the end of the promenade almost as far as the enormous Redcliffe Hotel. The still mild night made it a pleasant walk.

'They've spent a fortune on the pier recently. It's a real asset now. When I was a child it was a bit tacky,' remarked Mandy as they walked back towards the car parked on the seafront.

They rested briefly in a shelter and watched the incoming tide reach the sea wall as the almost full moon lit up the night sky. Peter put his arm around Mandy and kissed her for the first time. He could feel her responding as he pushed his tongue inside her mouth and his hand reached inside her coat to fondle her breasts. It was well past eleven before they got back to the car and Peter drove her home.

'Mum and Dad don't like me being out too late,' said Mandy as Peter parked his car outside her parents' house.

'This looks a very nice road to live in,' said Peter.

'Well, Dad's a very successful solicitor so he can afford a nice house; we've lived here for over ten years.'

Peter kissed her goodnight and walked to the front door. He gave a little skip as he returned to his car knowing he would be seeing her again in a couple of days for a drink in a Torquay pub.

A few days later Peter drove to the Berry Head Country Park and parked his car in the car park next to the visitors centre. They then walked the two miles back to Brixham town centre along the beautiful wooded coastal path.

'Isn't there a swimming pool somewhere in this area?' asked Mandy as they passed the halfway point.

'That's Shoalstone pool over there,' said Peter as the popular outdoor swimming pool, isolated on the exposed headland, came into view.

As they neared the town the harbour suddenly appeared in front of them. They stopped and found a seat to look at the wonderful views, across the open sea to Torquay. The congested harbour was packed with a variety of small craft shops as they passed the Golden Hind tourist attraction and turned towards the crowded pedestrianised shopping area in Fore Street just a few yards away.

'Let's find a nice place and have a cream tea,' suggested Peter as they came out of a souvenir shop.

The small, immaculate café was almost empty. The waitress delivered the scones, thick Devon clotted cream and strawberry jam to their table; the walking had made them hungry and thirsty and they soon demolished the scones.

'Do you want another cup of tea?' asked Mandy as she wiped cream and jam from her mouth with a tissue.

'Yes please,' said Peter as he scraped the last of the cream from the dish and put the spoon in his mouth.

'I'm not sure I should have eaten that last scone,' said Peter as he sat back in his chair feeling rather full.

'Are we walking back the same way we came?' asked Mandy.

'No, let's walk back along Berry Head Road, it runs parallel to the coastal path, unless you're too tired. We could get a taxi.'

She looked at him scornfully. 'We can't get a taxi, Peter, that would be cheating.'

The return journey was more uphill and they arrived back at the country park exhausted but with a sense of achievement.

Peter took Mandy to several pubs in the evenings. They didn't drink much but Peter enjoyed her company and her zest for life. He studied her approvingly as her deep affection for her parents and brother came across time and time again. Kay had been right when she said she was a super girl. She was that and much more besides.

Peter lay back in the bath and smiled to himself. He was delighted with the way his relationship with Mandy was developing. He had known her for a whole month and was now anxious to progress matters to the next stage. Tonight she would be driving round to his house and had volunteered to cook them dinner. He planned to try and persuade her to stay the night with him, or at least long enough for them to make love. He pondered on how responsible he had been in waiting a whole month before he tried to seduce her. He didn't usually wait that long but Mandy was different from most of the girls he had known. She was kind, pretty, loving and always thinking of other people. He let his mind race ahead. What more could any man want in a marriage partner? He finished his ablutions and stepped out of the bath. Good grief, was that the time? Mandy would be arriving in a few minutes and he wanted to be looking his best.

Mandy arrived wearing a pretty pink blouse and tight black trousers. Peter, now attired in an open-necked green short-sleeved shirt and expensive brown well-cut slacks, greeted her warmly with a long kiss and a hug. Mandy parked herself on the settee in the living room and smiled at him.

'You keep this house very neat and tidy for a man.'

'That sounds a bit sexist, Mandy.'

'Oh sorry, I shouldn't have said that. I didn't bring any food with me so I hope you've got plenty of food for me to choose from.'

'Well, I think I'm reasonably well stocked up. Come and see for yourself.'

She followed him to the kitchen and made straight for the fridge freezer. Peter watched her investigate the contents with considerable amusement. She seemed to be having difficulty making a decision.

'I told you I had plenty of supplies in.'

After a couple of minutes she announced her decision. 'You are having plaice, chips and peas. Have you any soup?'

He pointed to a large cupboard. She opened it.

'Right, we can start with chicken soup. How does all this suit you?'

'Fine, Mandy. It could be better than going to a restaurant.'

'If you're going to be cheeky you can cook yourself,' said Mandy, smiling at him.

'If you're still hungry, Peter, you can have tinned peaches and cream.'

Peter did not respond as he suspected that by the time they got to the sweet course he might have more important things on his mind. He decided to leave Mandy to it and went into the living room and started to watch the BBC One news.

'Have you got any napkins?' he heard her ask as the news headlines started.

He shouted back at her. 'No, I haven't, should I have? I've got some paper handkerchiefs, will they do?'

He couldn't quite make out what she was saying but he gathered she was not entirely happy with his answer. The news was coming to an end when the smells coming from the kitchen tempted him to go and see for himself what was going on. Mandy looked to have everything under control and she was pouring the soup into two dishes.

'Sit down, Peter, I'm ready. What have you got to drink?'

He went to the fridge and opened the door. 'I've got lager and some diet Pepsi. I'm having the beer.'

'Give me the Pepsi, please,' said Mandy as she placed two bowls of steaming hot soup on the kitchen table.

The meal was delicious. Peter not only had some peaches and tinned cream but actually took the initiative and made the coffee to complete the meal. He drew the line at tackling the washing-up – that could wait until tomorrow.

Peter had already reached under Mandy's blouse and removed her bra, without protest, and they kissed passionately on the settee, but as soon as he started to undo the belt of her trousers he felt her become anxious.

'I don't want to become pregnant, Peter.'

'Don't worry, I've got some condoms.'

Her resistance crumbled as he kissed her again on the lips and then lifted her up in his arms and carried her into the bedroom. She removed her blouse while Peter concentrated on her trousers closely followed by her small red panties. She was lovely! Small but perfectly rounded breasts, smooth soft skin, a trim figure and an inviting blonde triangle of pubic hair. He tore at the belt of his trousers and quickly pulled them off as Mandy helped take off his shirt. He was already fully erect as he removed his briefs and moved on top of her kissing and sucking her hard nipples.

As they lay exhausted in bed Peter kissed her gently on the lips. He couldn't remember when he had enjoyed sex so much and he was delighted he had made her come and satisfied her. He was looking forward to going inside her again as soon as he had a few minutes to recover. Unfortunately Mandy had other priorities.

'I can't stay the night with you, Peter, as much as I'd like to. My parents wouldn't like it and I don't want to upset them.'

'Oh, I was hoping you could stay. I was planning to cook you egg and bacon for breakfast.' She leant over and smiled at him, kissing him on the top of his nose.

'Thanks, but I can't stay.' She jumped out of bed and started dressing. Peter watched her intently, an idea forming in his mind.

'Mandy, would you like me to take you to the country on Saturday? We could have lunch at a nice restaurant, stay out all day and come back in the evening. It might be fun.'

Mandy finished hooking up her bra and turned to face him a look of pleasure and happiness written all over her face.

'That would be lovely! Can we start immediately after breakfast, say about nine thirty?'

'I don't see why not. Let's make a long day of it. I'll pick you up at nine thirty sharp.'

She rushed over to him, kissed him firmly on the lips and then hurriedly looked for her coat.

'See you on Saturday, Peter. Look at the time, it's nearly eleven thirty! I must fly; Mum and Dad will be getting worried. Can you phone Mum and tell her I'm on my way? She won't go to bed until I get back.'

'Consider it done, Mandy.' He blew her a kiss as she picked up her handbag ready to leave.

Peter got out of bed, put on his dressing gown and phoned Mandy's mum.

'She's got a bit delayed with the cooking – you know how it is,' said Peter.

He had a horrible feeling that Mandy's mum had not got total confidence in him but still she was relieved to know her daughter would be home in a few minutes.

Peter went to the kitchen to make himself a cup of coffee. He felt very pleased with himself. Mandy, he felt, was already head over heels in love with him. He liked her a lot and now that he had seen her performance in bed he was more convinced than ever that she was the girl he wanted to marry. She loved children as well – just as he did. Hopefully she would get pregnant as soon as they got married. A boy first, closely followed by a little girl. He wanted a large family so he hoped she wouldn't want to stop there. Mandy, he felt certain of this, would make a wonderful mother for his children. He was nearly twenty-nine and it was time for him to settle down.

What could conspire to spoil his well thought out plans? Perhaps an act of God but how could anyone legislate for that. Briefly he contemplated the possibility that he could remain faithful to Mandy and not lust after other women but it was only a passing thought and he quickly dismissed it from his mind.

Saturday dawned, chilly but sunny, ideal for an autumn drive in the lovely Devon and Somerset countryside. Mandy was smiling and ready and eager for the adventure to start when Peter arrived on her doorstep punctually, at the prearranged time. He noticed she was ideally dressed for the stiff October wind, in sensible trousers and stylish boots.

'I assume we are going to do some walking so I thought I would come prepared,' she cheerfully informed him as she greeted him at the front door.

'You've done the right thing, Mandy.'

'Where exactly are we going?'

'That's a surprise, for the moment, but I can tell you we're going close to Exeter and then on to the M5.'

'I like surprises,' replied Mandy.

With perfect manners and timing he walked round the front of his blue Escort and opened the passenger door for her.

'I want this to be a day we both remember for ever,' said Peter as he closed the door for her. He noticed a nervous smile cross her face as if he had said something totally unexpected. Peter felt surprised as well. Why had he said that? He felt embarrassed and disconcerted. *Surely*, he wondered, as he started the car, *he was not falling in love with Mandy*.

'Mum wanted to know if you were taking me anywhere dangerous.'

Peter hooted with laughter. 'She probably thinks being in the car with me is the dangerous bit. Let's not worry about your mum until we get home. Did you tell her we might be late?'

'Expect me when you see me, I said, but she knows I won't be too late.'

As Peter drove over the Devon border into Somerset heading towards the soft beauty of Exmoor, he could feel the warmth and excitement coming from Mandy as she talked non-stop about the beautiful countryside and the exquisite and dramatic autumn colours.

'Tell me where we're going, Peter. I can see we're in Somerset but I can't stand the suspense.'

'I know a lovely restaurant in Exford, right in the heart of Exmoor. My parents took my sister and me there years ago but I haven't been back since. Shall we see if the food is still good?' He looked over at Mandy, to see her reaction, and saw a huge smile light up her face.

'Sounds fine to me.'

As they stepped out of the car the brisk cool autumn wind stung their faces.

'I think we're going to need our coats,' said Peter as he opened the boot of the car. He looked at Mandy and he could see from the expression on her face that the beauty of the village entranced her.

'Let's have a walk around the village first, it's a bit early for lunch,' urged Peter.

They walked slowly past the village square and glanced in the windows of a couple of tourist shops. Already a sprinkling of visitors wandered the immaculate streets taking photographs and admiring the unspoilt beauty.

'We should have brought a camera, Peter. Look how beautiful the trees are at this time of year.'

'Yeah, we should have done. I've got a film to use up as well.'

'My parents always used to take Bobby and me to Dartmoor – never Exmoor,' said Mandy.

'After lunch, Mandy, I'm going to take you to the sea. The visibility is good today so we should be able to see the Welsh coast clearly,' replied Peter.

'That sounds exciting.'

'I've brought my binoculars – they're in the glove compartment. All this walking is making me ravenous, let's go and have some lunch,' said Peter.

Peter was greatly relieved to find that the cuisine at the pub restaurant was still of high standard. They both started with the homemade vegetable soup, which was delicious, with home-baked crusty white bread. Peter had a lager and lime and Mandy chose diet Pepsi. Peter, after much indecision, settled for homemade steak pie, while Mandy immediately opted for roast pork and apple sauce. The size of the portions took their breath away!

'I'm never going to be able to finish all this,' protested Mandy as she grinned at him.

'Do your best, darling,' replied Peter, now feeling faintly embarrassed as he realised he had probably used the word for the first time in his life. They ate in silence as the restaurant gradually filled up. Mandy pushed her plate aside with a heavy sigh as the last roast potato proved beyond her.

'I feel like I'm going to burst but I might be able to find room for a small portion of chocolate ice cream, Peter. How about you?' Mandy said as she studied the menu and passed it to Peter.

'Well, finishing all that pastry was a bit of a struggle but if you're having something perhaps I'll try some strawberry ice cream.'

'We are greedy,' ventured Mandy trying, unsuccessfully, to suppress a giggle.

They lingered quietly over coffee, watching the wind rustling the trees and the dead leaves falling gently to the ground.

'We were lucky to get this table by the window, weren't we, Peter?'

He smiled at her. 'Luck didn't come into it much really.'

'What do you mean?' asked Mandy, looking intrigued.

'I booked it yesterday.'

'Did you? That was clever of you. I'm very impressed.'

Peter said nothing but averted his eyes and gazed contentedly out of the window. After thanking the staff for an excellent meal and signing for his credit card it was time to leave. Peter left a generous tip and they set off for the car park.

'It's really fantastic here, Peter. I'd love to come back again soon, preferably with a camera. Can we?' enthused Mandy with a touch of excitement in her voice.

'Of course we can, but the day is still young and there's lot's more for us to see. Our next port of call is Minehead.'

'Isn't that where the big Butlin's holiday camp is?' asked Mandy.

'Yes, but there's far more to Minehead than that. You wait and see.'

The picturesque small West Somerset town was a delight. They managed to park in the main street and spent a few minutes looking at the shops, which were still busy with locals and visitors. Above the town towered North Hill and soon Peter had driven to the top of it. They jumped out of the car and looked across the Bristol Channel and saw the clear outline of the Welsh coast.

'Let me have a look,' said Mandy as Peter adjusted the focus on his binoculars. He handed them to her.

'What can you see?' asked Peter.

'Not much. I can see a lot of smoke belching out of some large chimneys. It looks much nicer this side,' said Mandy, handing back the binoculars.

Peter carefully folded up the strap and put them back in the case. He pointed across the water.

'Directly opposite us, according to this map, is Llantwit Major.

The holiday resort of Barry is about ten miles to the east but it looks as though we can't see that. Cardiff must be nearly ten miles to the north-east of Barry.' He started to make further calculations with his finger.

'If you travel by road from here it must be almost eighty miles to Llantwit Major.'

'Why don't they have a ferry?' asked Mandy.

'Not enough demand, I expect. This part of the country is very sparsely populated. Mind you it would be lot quicker.'

They fell into silence as they looked again across the water. Peter suddenly felt nervous. *Was this*, he wondered, *an opportune moment to broach the subject that had been preying on his mind ever since they had made love, for the first time, a few days before.*

'Mandy, can I ask you something?'

'Of course. What is it? You look so serious.'

'Well, I was just wondering… just wondering, now that we are seeing a lot of each other, can I ask you not to see anyone else?'

He looked straight into her eyes, eagerly awaiting a response. He was surprised to see a puzzled expression appear on her face.

'Why have you asked me that? I wouldn't dream of going out with anyone else while I'm going out with you.'

'That's fine,' replied Peter nervously. 'I hope you didn't mind me asking?' Seeing her unease, he quickly changed the subject. 'Let's see how this car tackles Porlock Hill. Then we can travel through the Valley of the Rocks as far as Lynton and then turn south and do a spot of shopping in Barnstaple. Look, this is the way we are going.'

She looked over his shoulder as he drew the line on the map with his forefinger.

'How does that sound, Mandy?' He saw a winsome smile light up her face.

'Let's go,' she responded, quickly breaking into a run as she raced him to the car.

The Escort negotiated the three-in-one steep gradient of Porlock Hill impressively and the magical journey along the northern tip of Exmoor and then down to Barnstaple was completed in less than an hour. The glorious scenery and autumnal colours made it a riveting experience. Peter parked in a council car park in the thriving North Devon town and fed the meter for a brief stay. They returned within half an hour with Mandy now the proud owner of six pretty tea towels decorated with Exmoor beauty spots.

'I can give them as presents,' said Mandy as Peter drove out of the car park.

Peter knew that the long winding road between Barnstaple and Crediton could be frustrating if you were in a hurry. Luckily they had all the time in the world as they embarked on the first part of their return journey to the English Riviera. The traffic was relatively light and they made reasonable progress.

'It's a good job we started early, we'll have done about two hundred miles by the time we get back to Torquay,' said Peter as they entered Crediton and easily found a parking space.

'I could do with a cuppa,' said Mandy as she stepped out of the car. The sun was about to disappear below the horizon as they walked down the attractive main street searching for a café.

'The clocks go back tonight,' said Mandy as one came into view.

Peter was hungry again and wanted more than a cup of tea. 'Let's go in here and have some sandwiches,' he said.

They asked for ham sandwiches and a pot of tea but the sandwiches turned out to be a disappointment.

'Are you sure you don't want more to eat than that?' asked Peter as Mandy pecked suspiciously at a rather dry ham sandwich.

'I had enough at lunchtime to last me a week,' replied Mandy, laughing.

'Well, I'm starving again. If you don't want those sandwiches hand them over to me.'

'What I was dying for was a cup of tea. Please pass me the milk, Peter, I'm absolutely parched.'

She poured out a second cup of tea and then stretched over to fill Peter's cup. Peter was grateful for it to wash down the rather unappetising ham sandwiches.

The café was deserted as they finished off their tea. The owner had changed the sign and it was now closed.

'I think he wants to close up,' Mandy said quietly.

'Why are you whispering, Mandy? Speak up, I can't hear what you're saying.' He noticed her cheeks were looking a little flushed. She seemed a trifle embarrassed.

'Quiet, Peter, he'll hear us. I said he wants to close the café.'

Peter looked round just to confirm her suspicions.

'Oh sorry, you should have said something earlier.'

They said a cheery goodnight to the man and left.

The daylight had almost gone as they entered the street. The cold night air made them shiver and Peter put his arm around Mandy to keep her warm as they hurried back to the car.

'Tomorrow it will be getting dark just after five. I always hate it when the clocks go back,' said Mandy.

'They should leave the clocks alone... it's a waste of time changing them,' asserted Peter.

'We seem to agree on a lot of things, Peter. We think the same way.'

The moon produced some light but the chilly wind made it abundantly clear that winter was just around the corner. The moon disappeared behind a dark cloud and the wind started to pick up, scattering the leaves and the litter left behind by the shoppers. The street was almost deserted as they returned to the car, keen to get home.

'Thanks for a lovely day, Peter, I've had a great time,' said Mandy as they reached the outskirts of Torquay.

'I've been to several places I've never been to before. We both like the countryside so much,' said Mandy.

'Yes, I've had a great time as well, especially being with you,' said Peter, looking across at her.

They noticed a few specks of rain appear on the windscreen followed almost immediately by a flash of forked lightning several miles to the south over Brixham.

'Let's get you home before this sets in,' Peter said as the rain got heavier.

'They said we might get a storm drifting in from the Channel late in the day,' said Mandy.

'For once they seem to be right. Thunderstorms in October! Look at it... pouring with rain and pitch black. Perhaps we're going to have a very bad winter, Mandy.'

Chapter Two

Peter had a surprise in store for Mandy and he could hardly wait to tell her. Her mother answered the door, poker faced and unsmiling, and ushered him into the living room. A strong aroma of roast beef filtered through from the kitchen and made Peter lick his lips in anticipation. Mandy was sitting on the floor, holding a pen, with writing paper resting on a magazine lying on the carpet.

'Hello, Mandy, you seem to be busy.'

'Hi Peter, I'm just finishing a letter to my brother at Durham University. He's been back a few weeks now so I thought I'd let him know what's going on.'

'My sister rang on Friday,' announced Peter. 'I told her about you. She wants us to go and visit them.'

'Okay, that's fine. When does she want us to go?'

'She suggested next weekend. I said I'd ask you today. They live in Bishop's Stortford. My brother-in-law is a customs officer at Stansted Airport. They live only a couple of miles from the airport so it's very convenient,' he continued, hardly pausing for breath. 'I know it's a long way to go but could you take a day off work on Friday. Then we could start back on Sunday afternoon. I really want to go. What do you think?'

Mandy took an age, or so it appeared to him, to reply.

'Well, I do have a couple of days owing. I'll ask tomorrow but I'm not sure that Mum and Dad are going to like this very much.'

'Tell them we'll be in separate beds,' suggested Peter, smiling at her.

'Shush, Peter, they'll hear you. I'm sure we won't be in separate beds and I'm not going to tell them fibs. Leave things to me – I'll talk to them later.'

Peter's face broke into a broad smile. The trip was on!

The roast beef and Yorkshire pudding were scrumptious. Despite his serious reservations about her – he was convinced she didn't like

15

him at all – Mandy's mum certainly knew how to cook Sunday lunch.

'Would you like some more Brussel sprouts, Peter?' she asked him.

'No thanks, but I will have another roast potato, please.'

He enjoyed the fruit salad and vanilla ice cream as well. What a pity, he thought as he wiped his mouth with a serviette, that most of the time she was such a miserable old cow. Mandy, he knew, thought the world of her so he would have to be careful what he said.

Peter let his thoughts leap to next weekend. He knew the Sunday lunch would be just as good as today. It would be great to see Jane and Steve again to show Mandy off and see the little ones, Zoe and Jason.

The wind howled across Torbay as Friday dawned, cold and stormy. Peter, still half-asleep switched on the television and turned to Ceefax. He was relieved to see that the wind was due to abate in the next few hours. Meanwhile, it seemed that the south-east had not suffered to the same degree. He weighed up the pros and cons. The forecast was for better weather later but judging by the noise outside there was a gale blowing at the moment. He decided it was probably not as bad as it sounded. He located his mobile phone and rang Mandy. Her father answered.

'It's blowing hard here, Peter, I don't think you ought to go.'

'The forecast says it will get better in a few hours. Can I speak to Mandy?'

'Hello, Peter, what's it like where you are?'

'It's not too bad, Mandy. The weather reports say it will be much better later in the day. Let's take a chance!'

'Dad's been out, there's a tree down at the end of our road but cars can still get through. It's blowing a gale here.'

'Well, you're a bit exposed there. Here it's only a very strong wind and I'm sure it will improve.'

'All right then, I'll finish packing. See you in a few minutes.'

Peter rushed to have some toast and a cup of tea before completing his packing. In no time he was ready and he opened the front door with his suitcase in his hand. The wind nearly knocked him off his feet!

Leaving Torquay was not as straightforward as Peter had hoped. The overnight gales had brought chaos. Many trees were down and Torbay Council workmen were everywhere. Mandy, Peter noticed, seemed completely unperturbed.

'Dad wasn't too pleased that we're going but I managed to calm him down.'

'Good, I'm relieved to hear that.'

'Isn't this exciting?' said Mandy as the wind shook the car.

They finally cleared Torbay and made their way steadily through Kingskerswell towards Newton Abbot.

'Don't worry, we'll be fine as long as an enormous tree doesn't fall on the car and squash us flat as pancakes,' said Peter. He looked at Mandy and they both burst out laughing as if they didn't have a care in the world.

'Mum and Dad say you're irresponsible. I must ring them later on your mobile and tell them we're okay.'

They stared at a high-sided lorry that had been blown on to its side but otherwise the road was clear.

'Which way are we going?' enquired Mandy, stifling a yawn, as they neared Exeter with the gale-force winds easing slightly.

'I thought it might be quicker to go on the A30 now that the new section is open near Honiton. It's a far more attractive route as well.'

'Fine,' replied Mandy sleepily. She adjusted her seat into the reclining position, closed her eyes and dozed off. She woke later with a start.

'Where are we, Peter?'

'Near Wincanton on the 303. You've been asleep for ages. You've missed all the best scenery.'

'My mouth is as dry as a bone and my neck hurts,' replied Mandy, a picture of misery as she wiped the sleep from her eyes.

'There's a bottle of water inside the glove compartment.'

'Oh, that's good, Peter, you think of everything.' She took a long drink and then offered the bottle to Peter. He waved it aside.

'I'm going to stop in about half an hour. Keep your eyes open for a nice place. You were snoring very loudly a short time ago,' added Peter, innocently.

Mandy sat up straight, now wide awake. 'I don't snore. You pig, take that back!'

'Only joking, darling.' He looked across at her and started to laugh. He was delighted to see a beautiful smile light up her face.

'There's a Little Chef coming up, Peter, do you want to stop?'

Peter slowed down.

'Yes, that looks quite nice. We'll stop here for a bit. We're only a few miles from Stonehenge.'

The wind was still strong and cold but thankfully the gale force winds and driving rain had relented. They still hurried inside to keep warm. The Christmas decorations, already on view although it was only the end of November, welcomed them as they ordered buttered toasted teacakes, and a pot of tea.

'What time do you think we'll arrive?' asked Mandy as she poured out the tea. Peter consulted his watch.

'It's a quarter past eleven now. We might get there soon after two but it all depends on the M25. Hopefully we won't have to stop again.'

Mandy looked thoughtful as she finished her tea. 'The last year seems to have flown by, especially the last few months. Thanks for being so nice to me.'

Peter felt the urge to lean across the table and plant a huge kiss on those inviting lips but he felt inhibited by a large boisterous family occupying the table next to them. However, as they left, he made sure he held her hand tightly.

The M25 near Heathrow was slow and frustrating, but once clear of this the traffic thinned out and they made good progress. Soon they were on the final straight as they joined the M11. They hardly noticed the rich, flat Essex farmland as they neared their destination. It was a few minutes after two when Peter veered off the motorway towards the prosperous growing town of Bishop's Stortford, on the Hertfordshire–Essex border. The weather had changed beyond all recognition from when they had started out. Late autumn Devon gales and angry sky had been replaced by a brisk wind and broken rain-free clouds.

'We certainly made the right decision in coming,' said Peter as they drove past the golf club on the way to the town centre.

'How old are the children?' Mandy asked.

'Zoe's five and Jason three and a half. I'm sure you'll find them a bit of a handful. I know Jane does.'

'Don't worry, I love children. I'm sure we'll get on famously.'

Peter was pleased to see that her prediction turned out to be correct. The sweets that Mandy had brought with her turned out to be the perfect icebreaker. They were clambering all over her as she lifted them up alternately and planted kisses all over their faces. Their uncle, Peter, noticed with just a trace of jealousy, hardly got any attention at all.

Jane had been working hard in the kitchen preparing a late lunch.

'Leave Mandy alone, and let her have something to eat,' insisted Jane as the rest of the adults tucked into a ham salad and new potatoes.

'Aren't the kids having anything?' asked Peter.

'We had spam and chips, then banana and custard,' said Zoe.

'They had their lunch hours ago,' said Jane.

'What sort of journey did you have?' asked Steve.

'Rough at the start,' replied Peter. 'I think there's quite a bit of structural damage. The wind was ferocious; you could hardly stand up and it was touch and go whether we came at all. But once we passed Exeter Airport the rain suddenly stopped and the wind eased off.'

'Well, it's lovely to see you both and the kids seem very pleased as well,' said Jane as she cleared the plates ready for the apple crumble and cream.

'I expect the kids will want some crumble,' said Steve as he fetched extra dishes,

'How's the job at the insurance agency?' enquired Steve.

'Fine – I've been manager there for almost two and a half years now. We keep picking up new business and holding on to most of our existing clients. I'm very pleased at the moment, touch wood! How's the airport?'

'Still expanding. I earn a reasonable amount of money but it's a bit of a rat race at times. Sometimes I think it would be nice to live in your part of the world but at thirty-two that dream is a long way off.'

The meal was barely finished before the children requested that Mandy accompany them upstairs to carry out an inspection of their toys in the playroom. Zoe caught hold of her hand and pulled her towards the stairs. Mandy was full of enthusiasm and carried Jason up the stairs. Peter watched and felt proud of her.

Squeals of delight reverberating from upstairs were swiftly followed by sounds of children squabbling over the ownership of toys. Mandy, acting as peacemaker, soon restored harmony and the rest of the afternoon went like clockwork. Later, after a noisy supper, both Jason and Zoe refused to go to sleep until Mandy had read them a succession of stories; finally they succumbed to the inevitable and fell asleep an hour after their normal bedtime.

Mandy slumped exhausted into a chair as she joined the others watching television in the living room.

'I can't see you being fit enough to go to work on Monday, Mandy,' said Steve.

'Rubbish! Don't talk nonsense. Where are we taking them tomorrow?' Mandy asked, clearly not daunted by the considerable demands being put on her.

'The forest is very nice and they love it there,' said Steve.

'Good idea,' agreed Peter. 'You'll like it there as well, Mandy.'

Saturday morning was clear with only a light breeze. The excited children were dressed in warm winter coats, trousers, gloves and Wellington boots. They sensed an adventure and Zoe had shrieked loudly when told they were going to the forest.

'Daddy's gone to work so he won't be able to come with you today, darling,' said Jane.

Zoe looked unconcerned. *Why should she worry*? Peter thought, *after all she had a new guardian angel to look after her now.*

'I'm going to do a lot of housework and then make you lunch,' announced Jane. 'I'm sure you'll all be starving after your walk.'

'Mummy, can we have fish fingers for lunch?' Zoe pestered.

'All right, you and Jason can have fish fingers but the grown-ups are having corned beef. Everyone is having baked beans, darling. Is that all right?'

'Yes, Mummy, as long as I can have more than anybody else.'

Hatfield Forest was only a couple of miles from Bishop's Stortford – over the boundary of Hertfordshire into Essex. A relatively unspoilt area ideal for walking, horse riding or exercising dogs. Now almost bare as winter inexorably approached, it was still an attractive location. Only a few months earlier, in late summer, blackberries had blanketed many parts of the forest, luring those willing to risk the sharp pain of the thorns as they gathered in the juicy black fruit. Only the persistent drone of planes disturbed the tranquillity.

Peter parked his Escort near the main entrance and quickly unbuckled the children and bundled them out of the car. They were soon running, chasing each other and laughing together. Rabbits played in the open before scurrying into the bushes as the children interrupted their games.

A sombre picture overpowered them as they reached the lake. The scars left behind by the Korean cargo jet which had crashed eleven months before, killing all the crew, had clearly not healed. A huge crater remained where the doomed plane had finally come to rest, a vivid reminder of the calamity that had occurred. They pressed on deeper into the forest, the children oblivious to the tragedy, wrapped up in their own enchanting world, where Father Christmas still exists and heaven is having baked beans for lunch.

The children raced ahead. Their excited faces turning occasionally to see if the adults would reprimand them for going too far ahead. Peter looked across at Mandy. He wondered if she was thinking the same thing as he was. She smiled the same sweet smile that had mesmerised him several times before. He took hold of her arm and pulled her towards him and kissed her passionately, holding her as tightly as he could without hurting her. The tragedy, behind them, a reminder of the past. The future, chasing each other in the bushes, in front of them.

Within the hour they were back at base camp, the children tired but still active.

'That was really nice, Peter. We must take the kids there again when we next visit your sister.'

'Shall we take the kids shopping in the town centre?' asked Peter.

'We could buy presents,' replied Mandy.

A quick drink and the children were ready.

Jason had his face covered in chocolate ice cream. Zoe pointed this out continuously until the necessary action was taken, as Peter carried Jason along South Street in Bishop's Stortford town centre.

'Have you got a hankie, Uncle Peter? Look at the mess on Jason's face. I keep on asking.'

Peter stopped and Mandy delved into her handbag and triumphantly produced a paper handkerchief.

'Let me do it,' insisted Zoe.

Peter lowered Jason to the ground so that Zoe could get to work.

'Perhaps this is good training for the future,' suggested Peter as they started off again, the streets emptying fast as the last of the shoppers made their way home.

All agreed that the shopping expedition had been an unqualified success. Zoe was now in possession of a Barbie doll and Jason clutched lovingly at a rather odd-looking frog, now plastered with ice cream.

'Will it wash off?' asked a worried looking Zoe, gesticulating and pointing at the mess.

'I expect so, darling,' soothed Mandy gently, removing the remnants of the ice cream from Jason's grasp and efficiently depositing it in the nearest waste bin.

'Did you know that Cecil Rhodes was born in this town?' Peter asked.

'Who's Cecil Rhodes?' she replied, looking blankly at him.

'He was a famous statesman in Africa during the second half of the nineteenth century.'

She gave a little chuckle. 'Geography and history were never my strong points at school. Maths was my best subject. I got better grades than most of the boys.'

'Ah, now I know why you went to work in a bank. You're good at counting money.'

She smiled tolerantly at him. 'It's slightly more complicated than that.'

'Let's get these two home now, it's getting cold,' said Peter as they reached the car.

Peter parked the car outside Steve and Jane's house. The clock on the dashboard showed five past six.

'I bet you two are ready for tea,' said Mandy as she unbuckled Jason's seat belt. Their answers left no doubt that they were.

The red wine went well with the roast lamb, roast potatoes, carrots, broccoli and mint sauce. The little ones were content with burger and chips washed down with orange squash.

'These kids have made us absolutely ravenous,' said Peter as he reached for a second helping of potatoes with a large spoon.

'They are going to have a bath later on,' said Jane.

'Can Mandy do it?' Zoe asked, not totally unexpectedly.

'I expect so, darling, she seems to be doing most things for you at the moment,' Jane added to general amusement.

Bath time turned out to be noisy and wet.

'Zoe, we need to keep the water in the bath,' Mandy gently scolded as the little girl enthusiastically splashed more water onto the floor.

'Perhaps you put too much water in the bath,' suggested Peter who, up to this point, had been sitting on a chair in the corner of the room, minding his own business, reading that morning's newspaper.

'Don't talk, wet, Peter. Oh sorry, I didn't mean that.' They both laughed.

'Mummy is not going to be very pleased with this wet floor, Zoe,' said Mandy. Zoe remained silent but kept her arms still.

'How do you like school?'

'All right.'

'Who are your friends?' Mandy persisted.

'Holly, Sarah and Josie are my best friends. I like David as well.'

'That's good. What's your teacher's name?'

'Miss Scott.'

'Is she nice?'

'Yes,' Zoe replied and then hesitated, 'but she stops us talking.'

'Right, children, I think it's time you were out of the bath. Peter, can you take your head out of that paper and pass me a towel. You dry Jason and I'll do Zoe,' said Mandy.

Peter suddenly found himself galvanised into action. He tossed a bright yellow towel in the general direction of the bath. It landed on Jason's head and rolled into the water before Mandy could grab it. Zoe screamed with delight! Mandy was less pleased. Jason pushed the towel under the water.

'Perhaps you could pass it to me next time.'

'Sorry, Mandy, but it's a big bathroom.'

The following day, the children were still fast asleep even though it was nine thirty in the morning. The exertions and excitement of the previous two days had taken their toll. Peter and Mandy opened the front door as carefully as possible, anxious not to wake them. Now they would have some time to themselves but would see them all again at lunchtime.

Peter took the same road as he had done the previous day but this time didn't turn off to the forest. They passed through the village of Little Hallingbury and then, a mile further on, stopped at the village stores in the larger village of Hatfield Heath, so that Peter could buy a copy of *The Sunday Times*. He drove on a few miles until they reached the delightful village of Matching Green and parked on the enormous green, where on summer weekends the place was alive with the sound of cricket. They walked hand in hand across the grass – the affluence apparent everywhere they looked.

'Those houses must cost a fortune,' said Mandy wistfully as they looked around them.

'I think you're right – it's probably best not to think about it. We will never be able to afford one unless we win the lottery. Let's get back to the car. We can carry on along this road and then come back in a circle.'

Peter drove on a mile or so until they came to Matching Tye and then three miles on to Old Harlow. Peter then turned right to return to Hatfield Heath passing through the village of Sheering.

The strong smell of steak and kidney pie greeted them as they opened the front door on their return.

'I hope there's time for me to finish packing before lunch,' said Mandy.

'It will be about fifteen minutes,' replied Jane.

'That's probably enough time.'

Mandy rushed upstairs with Zoe scampering close behind her. Peter joined Jane in the kitchen. For a moment they were alone.

'Mandy is wonderful with the children, Peter, she's a lovely girl.'

'I know – it could be serious this time. I'm very lucky to have met her.'

'You've had so many girlfriends over the last ten years. You're a wandering eye,' said Jane.

'You don't think I'd be silly enough to jeopardise a relationship with her by messing about with other women. I'm mad about her.'

'I'm pleased to hear that. I still get upset when I think what Dad did to Mum.'

'Like father, like son, you mean. No, I'm not that silly, Jane. Trust me!'

'Thanks for a great weekend, Jane,' said Peter as he lifted one of the bags into the boot.

'I can't see Mandy.'

'She's upstairs with the kids. They seem reluctant to let her go. I'll go inside and tell her you're ready to leave.'

'The traffic shouldn't be too bad today,' suggested Steve, 'but I don't like the look of that sky, Peter.'

Mandy arrived and fastened her seatbelt.

'I've got a horrible feeling we're going to have a lousy winter,' said Peter, making a face. He turned the engine on and, as usual, it started first time.

'See you all again soon,' said Peter as he let the handbrake off.

The children waved until the car was out of sight. It had been a marvellous weekend.

Chapter Three

They approached the town centre split-level multi-storey car park from Abbey Road. Mandy had volunteered to drive her Mini and Peter always felt confident when she was driving. They knew, as it was the last Saturday before Christmas, that they needed to arrive early, otherwise the car park would be full. Peter was in good spirit as he jumped out of the car to feed the ticket machine.

'Will four hours be enough?' he questioned as Mandy finished parking.

'Yes, I should think so, Peter.'

He had asked her the big question and she had said yes. Now armed with his credit card, he was eager to buy Mandy an engagement ring – just in time for Christmas.

He had been thinking of asking her for several weeks and had briefly hesitated because he had only been going out with her for three months. He knew he was now madly in love with her. It was crucial and significant, he felt, that during the whole three months he had not been tempted to seduce any other woman. It was true that he still liked to look but the urge to touch seemed to have disappeared. Was this a temporary phenomenon or was the leopard changing his spots? He liked to think it might be the latter but only time would tell. He had never felt this way about anybody before. Also the sex with Mandy was still exciting. She liked to experiment, as he did, and was always eager to please.

They decided not to bother with the lift as a small queue had formed. As they turned the corner into the covered passageway leading to the shops, Peter searched in his pocket for some loose change as he saw a busker sitting on the ground. They could already hear the Christmas music ahead.

Union Street was already heaving, although it was only ten thirty, when as they joined the throng in Torquay's main street. They admired the huge Christmas tree and the array of lights and seasonal decorations.

'Is that the real Father Christmas over there or an impostor?' asked Peter to Mandy's delight.

The mild weather encouraged the younger element to discard their coats as the winter sun broke through and allowed the temperature to climb into the mid-fifties. Mandy was keen to start looking.

'That shop looks nice,' said Mandy after a brief period of window shopping. They looked at the window display. Some expensive rings stared back at them.

'Shall we go inside and try some on?' said Peter. Nothing was too good for Mandy, he had decided.

'Shall we?' responded Mandy, almost shyly.

'Well, we won't find what we're looking for if we stand out here in the street,' responded Peter with a note of exasperation creeping into his voice.

They ventured nervously inside. A tall, thin man was very polite and helpful and produced an inviting tray of rings from the window display. Mandy inspected them carefully. Peter's bravado started to wane as he was reasonably confident she would not choose one of the most expensive ones. She pointed at the ring she liked. The man slowly pushed it onto her finger and smiled. It was almost a perfect fit. She waggled her finger up and down and it didn't fall off. She gazed at it long and hard with a serious expression on her face. She took it outside to look at it in the daylight and she returned smiling.

'I like it, Peter.'

He felt relieved. This one was almost the cheapest!

'It's not too expensive, is it?' asked Mandy.

'No, that's fine. Do you really like it?'

Her face broke into a perfect smile. 'It's gorgeous. Thank you darling – let's buy it.'

They celebrated later, after buying a few presents, with two enormous pizzas supplemented with Coca Cola.

'I hope my dad likes those slippers. At least I know his size,' said Mandy as she started to make hard work of the second half of her ham and pineapple pizza.

'I usually hate shopping but it's been fun today,' said Peter, passing his plate towards Mandy as it became clear she had finally given up the unequal struggle with the pizza. She deposited the rest of it onto Peter's plate.

'I'm not sure how many people we should invite to our engagement party,' said Mandy.

'If we hold it in my house I can accommodate about twenty-five,' said Peter.

'Your house is not that big, you know.'

'Yes, it is. I'm sure we can get that many in.' Mandy reached for her handbag and pulled out her diary.

'Saturday 20 January,' she suggested.

'Okay, that gives us several weeks to organise things. You can arrange the invites.'

'Right, if you give me a list of your friends in the next few days you can leave it all to me,' she reassured him.

'We won't invite the geriatrics – just our friends.'

'Are you calling my parents geriatrics?'

'For this party, yes.' He looked at her. She seemed a little disappointed. He tried to explain his reasoning. 'Most of the people will be our age. Some people are going to drink too much. The music will be very loud. Other things may be going on.'

'What other things, Peter?' she said, a note of concern creeping into her voice.

'Well… well, you know.'

'No, I don't know. What do you mean? Are you talking about drugs?'

'Some of my friends use cannabis – it's harmless.'

'It's also illegal,' responded Mandy. 'I don't want any drugs at our party. I'd rather not have a party at all than have drugs and that includes cannabis. Have you ever taken any drugs?'

Peter felt himself on the defensive. He thought it wise not to tell her the whole truth.

'I've tried cannabis – nothing else. There's no need for you to worry.' But he saw the concern written all over her face.

'Promise me you won't take any drugs,' entreated Mandy.

'Don't panic, Mandy, it was only on the odd occasion. Don't worry, darling, I'll make sure there are no drugs at our party. Trust me!' He could see from the look on her face that alarm bells were still ringing in her head. *Why*, he wondered, *hadn't he kept his big mouth shut?*

The New Year was not even a week old but Mandy was heartbroken. Although her grandmother had reached the venerable age of eighty-three she had been in relatively good health. But sudden complications, following a severe bout of flu, had resulted in a rapid deterioration in her condition. Mandy had been relieved to learn that she had died peacefully.

'She seemed to be coming down with it when we saw her on Christmas Day,' said Mandy when she phoned Peter to tell him. 'I'm going to miss her, Peter. I want you to come to the funeral.'

Peter took the afternoon off the following Thursday to drive Mandy to the funeral in Bovey Tracey.

'Granddad died four years ago. They lived happily at Bovey for nearly twenty years after he retired from the practice,' reminisced Mandy on the way.

'How did she get on, living on her own?' asked Peter.

'We asked her to come and live in Torquay when Granddad died, but she liked the house so much and the beautiful surroundings that we couldn't persuade her. They used to walk on Dartmoor for hours and sometimes they used to take me. I loved it. It was the Dartmoor ponies that I liked best. I used to take sugar lumps in my pocket. Now there are very few left. I think it's so sad.'

The journey took almost forty-five minutes.

'This must be one of the loveliest parts of Devon,' said Peter as he parked his car in the church car park near the centre of Bovey Tracey.

The church was about a third full and Peter put his arm around Mandy as she tearfully said goodbye to her favourite grandmother. The priest spoke eloquently.

'Today we say goodbye to a wonderful lady who will be sadly missed by all who knew her. During the Second World War she had to bring up her two children, Mary and Steven, alone, while her husband, Jack, was held prisoner by the Japanese in atrocious conditions for three long years. After the war she worked for many years as a nurse in Devon before their retirement to their beloved Dartmoor. Her husband, of course, after his release and a further six months to recuperate, resumed his career as a junior solicitor.'

Mandy wiped further tears from her eyes as Peter put his arm round her shoulder again.

Mandy's parents had stayed overnight in the house on the outskirts of Bovey Tracey. Most of the mourners now trouped back to the house for refreshments and solace. Mandy gave her mother a tearful hug and Peter felt himself lucky to avoid the same fate. They did not stay too long as Mandy was still upset.

Peter and Mandy sat in silence as they made their way back to

Torquay. This time he had taken the scenic route crossing part of Dartmoor including the popular and impressive peak of Haytor and then on towards Ashburton. They saw a few hardy Dartmoor ponies huddled together for warmth with their backs to the biting wind, as the brief warmth of the afternoon sun rapidly gave way to early evening frost.

'Dad says Grandma has left some money to me and Bobby,' announced Mandy as they entered the delightful village of Dartington, on the way to Totnes just a mile down the road.

'They were very well off. Dad says my share is £30,000.'

'That's quite a large sum.'

'I know. I think I'll put most of it in the building society. We're going to need a larger house if we have children.' Mandy looked across at him.

'That sounds like a very sensible idea,' replied Peter.

The last rays of sunshine were disappearing below the horizon as they entered Torquay from the ring road down Shiphay Lane.

'It's been a sad day, Peter,' said Mandy as he pulled up outside her parents' house. She leant over and kissed him lightly on the lips. 'See you tomorrow, darling,' she said as she closed the passenger door.

As he drove the mile to his house Peter was in a reflective mood. How lucky he was to have Mandy – in so many ways the girl of his dreams. He jammed the brakes on and stopped abruptly at a zebra crossing. Two pretty girls, probably Swedish from one of the language schools he guessed, crossed in front of him wearing short, provocative skirts. One looked directly into the car and smiled. He smiled back. *No harm in looking*, he thought. But Mandy was such an angel. Maybe in less than a year they would be married. Then perhaps she would be expecting and they would be planning for the new arrival.

Peter reached home and left his car in the driveway. He always liked to put the car away at night so he opened the garage door and drove the car inside. As he closed the door, a watery half-moon caught his eye. It felt cold – perhaps even in mild Torquay there would be a frost before dawn. Inside his body, however, he felt warm and snug. A sense of elatedness suddenly overwhelmed him. He was sure he wanted to marry her and make her happy. He locked the garage and opened the front door stopping for a moment before he closed it. He made himself a promise. When they returned to the house for the first time after their marriage, he was going to carry her over the threshold just like they did in the old black and white Hollywood movies.

The party had warmed up nicely and everyone seemed to be enjoying themselves. Most people had brought plenty of drink but Jim and Kay had excelled themselves by bringing champagne. The music, as Peter had predicted, was loud and incessant. Abba, Mandy's favourite group, prevailed and Peter hoped the neighbours were in a tolerant mood. Mandy couldn't believe there were only twenty-five people in the house and accused Peter of cheating.

'It's not my fault if there are one or two gatecrashers,' replied Peter in his defence. After a slow start the dancing had got under way, with Johnny, one of Peter's friends, leading the way. Many of the guests congregated in the kitchen as the living room proved hopelessly inadequate to accommodate everyone.

Mandy and Kay had prepared some appetising food. Hot sausage rolls, hot pizza, pineapple and cheese sticks, four varieties of sandwiches, peanuts and plain and smoky bacon crisps. All this followed by trifle, tinned fruit and ice cream.

'Does anyone else want a soft drink?' shouted Kay above the din as she emptied a cardboard box full of cartons of fresh orange juice and bottles of Coca Cola, which she had produced from the boot of her car.

'I knew everyone would bring booze,' said Kay.

'How many people want coffee?' asked Mandy. 'Could you go round and ask, Peter?'

'Anything you say, precious,' replied Peter, now starting to feel the effects of several lagers.

Jim opened the champagne at eleven thirty to loud applause. He threatened to behave like the winner of a motor racing Grand Prix but as the guests scattered he relented to save them from the deluge.

'Here's to Mandy and Peter – may all their troubles be little ones,' declared Jim as he lifted the sparkling white wine to his lips.

The laughter and groans had barely subsided when Jim eagerly thrust a full glass into Peter's hand to cries of 'Speech!' He made a slightly incoherent speech but nobody took much notice and he sat down to prolonged applause. He couldn't recall much after that!

Peter lay on the settee. He did not feel well at all. His vision was blurred but he could sense some people sitting on the other side of the room. He was almost sure one of them was Mandy.

'Peter, are you okay?'

He lay back, closed his eyes and felt safe again. That was definitely Mandy speaking. He'd know that voice anywhere but he couldn't understand why she was asking him silly questions.

'Peter, are you all right?' she cried, her voice becoming more urgent.

'Everyone has gone home except Jim and Kay. They're not drunk so why are you? Why did you have to drink all that champagne?'

Peter felt himself groan as he clasped his hands to his head. More silly questions. Why bother answering more silly questions. He felt a soothing hand on his forehead.

'Jim, can you help me carry him upstairs to bed?'

Peter felt vaguely resentful. He couldn't figure out why. He was very comfortable where he was, she should mind her own business and leave him in peace.

'You take his legs and I'll take the heavy end,' he heard Jim say to Mandy.

Good grief, even his friends were interfering now. He felt as if he was being taken in an upwards direction.

'Mind his head – you nearly hit it on that corner!' screeched Mandy.

Something inside his head told him he was in grave danger but, inexplicably, he could do nothing to save himself. Why wouldn't they leave him alone? After all, he only wanted to go to sleep. Surely that was not too much to ask.

'These trousers are tight,' complained Mandy as she struggled to pull them off. 'Can you help me, Kay?'

Peter felt light-headed but alert enough now to panic. What on earth was she doing? Perhaps she had gone mad!

'I'll leave you to take his briefs off,' said Kay thoughtfully.

Peter opened his mouth to say something but was overcome by another dizzy spell. He lay back, exhausted and defeated, unable to speak.

'What a state you're in,' was the last thing he heard Mandy say as he felt his eyelids getting heavier and heavier.

When he woke he was surprised to find her asleep beside him. He felt awful but managed to ease himself out of bed without waking Mandy and made a beeline for the bathroom cabinet. He soon found what he was looking for and hoped two Anadin would be enough to cure his splitting headache. What a party it must have been but unfortunately he couldn't remember much about it. He managed to get back into bed without waking Mandy and fell asleep again almost as soon as his head touched the pillow.

When he woke again he was alone. The pounding in his head was almost gone and downstairs he could hear some activity. It sounded as if it was coming from the kitchen. He decided to sit tight and see what developed. Very soon her pretty face appeared, looking anxiously round the bedroom door. She smiled when she saw that he was awake.

'How are you feeling, darling? Better than last night, I hope.'

'I don't feel too bad. I had some pills a couple of hours ago and they seem to have done the trick. Was it a good party, Mandy?'

'You don't remember. It was great. Everybody enjoyed themselves. It was probably a good idea not to invite the geriatrics though – they might have been shocked at your condition.'

He felt his face redden as he painfully recalled the humiliation of only a few hours before.

'I'll go down and make some strong coffee. Are you hungry?' asked Mandy.

He made a face at her.

'Just some orange juice Mandy please. Can you bring it up here?'

Soon she returned with breakfast served on a tray. She sat on the edge of the bed in his dressing gown as he started on the orange juice. She poured him a cup of coffee and had one herself. The juice tasted good and he finished it in a couple of gulps.

'That was the first night you've spent with me in this house.'

'So it was. I couldn't leave you, not in the state you were in. Mind you, it would have been difficult for you to have made love to me last night.'

She took the tray when he had finished and placed it on the dressing table. She returned and sat on the bed close to him.

'I've got nothing on under this, Peter. Perhaps you can make up for last night now.'

She stood up and pulled the cord gently. The dressing gown opened, revealing the body that still excited him. She sat down on the bed, in front of him, so that he could pull it off her shoulders. She slipped into bed beside him snuggling up close and kissed him on the mouth. Peter felt himself responding as he pulled her close feeling her firm breasts on his chest. They made love quietly and enjoyably. Afterwards Peter felt the need to talk.

'I think we should have several children,' he said as he looked into her eyes.

She smiled back at him. 'Let's start off with one and see how we get on,' she countered, laughing.

'Perhaps you'll be clever enough to have twins.'

'Now that would be a bit of a handful.'

'But it would be a lot quicker if we did it in twos.'

'Don't worry, I'm not twenty-five until June so there's plenty of time for us to have a large family if we want one.' Her face suddenly dropped as her mood changed. 'Sometimes I worry about bringing more children into the world. There seems to be so much evil about.'

Her melancholy gloom made him uneasy. He sought to lift her out of it.

'When do you want to get married?' He saw her face light up.

'October would be nice, darling. I want it to be in a church. Is that all right?'

'Yes fine. I'd like to get married in church as well. October is only nine months away so we'd better get our skates on.'

'It's going to cost a lot of money,' said Mandy.

'Your dad's a well-known solicitor in Torbay, Mandy, so he can probably afford it.'

'That's true. The practice is doing very well at the moment.'

'I just hope my parents are speaking to each other at the wedding. Relations have been awful since the divorce.'

'When was it?'

'Three years ago. It was pretty awful at the time.'

'Tell me more about what happened,' Mandy said.

Peter reflected on the traumatic events that had transformed his parents' lives.

'They had been married twenty-six years. They owned this hotel near Babbacombe Beach. Then my father embarked on an affair with Sonia, who was the daughter of another hotelier in Torquay. She was a bit of a stunner but was over twenty years younger than my father. My mother didn't find out for over six months and when she did all hell broke loose.'

'Really!' said Mandy, her eyes nearly popping out of her head.

'The affair didn't last very long after that but my mother never forgave him. She demanded a divorce. The hotel had to be sold and the proceeds divided up. That's why my father runs a taxi business and my mother lives in Totnes with my aunt.'

'Does Sonia still live in Torquay?'

'I don't know about that. I heard she got married last year.'

'I wonder if either of your parents will get married again.'

'My father might. He sees a widow in Paignton – she's over ten years younger than him. My mother probably won't marry again, but who knows. More and more people are living alone these days,' he observed philosophically.

'Your mother doesn't look terribly happy,' Mandy said with concern.

'Well, now you know the whole story you can see why. She liked running the hotel. Now I think she misses meeting people. My father is well and truly in the dog house as far as she's concerned.'

'Who's side were you on?'

'Neither really. Jane and I were "piggies in the middle".'

'But didn't you feel angry with your father? I know I would.'

'Not really, but I didn't want them to get divorced. I think she should have forgiven him and carried on as normal.'

'But he betrayed her,' insisted Mandy indignantly.

'Sure – but I don't think he was planning to leave her. What good has it done her anyway?' He looked at her but she said nothing.

'Don't you like my father, Mandy?'

'I didn't say that, Peter. We get on fine but I don't see much of him.'

'Don't worry, darling, I'm sure nothing like that will happen to us. You know how I feel about you.' He gave her a kiss on the cheek to reassure her.

She whispered in his ear. 'I love you, Peter. I don't want anything to spoil our happiness.'

He pulled her close to him again. Soon he felt drowsy and Mandy fell asleep with her head resting on his chest. They slept until lunchtime.

Chapter Four

Sue Read glanced at the line of birthday cards on the mantelpiece. Two had fallen over so she picked them up. One was from David. She read it again. 'Happy twenty-seventh birthday. I miss you. Love, David.' She wished he hadn't sent the card. Now, irritatingly, her conscience started to trouble her again as it had several times since the break-up the previous month. She gave a little sigh. *Why*, she wondered, *hadn't she put it straight in the bin?* Quickly her resolve hardened as she replaced the card in its original position. He was nice, kind and considerate but she knew she didn't want to marry him. The wife of an accountant would be safe but boring, she concluded. They had had some good times but it had all got so predictable. He would find someone else soon. She wanted to meet other people. It was over!

She gulped down a second cup of tea and dumped the dishes in the sink. The cuckoo clock on the wall told her it was almost time to go. She rushed into the bedroom and discarded her short blue skirt, tights and dark blue jumper. She reached for her brand new gold tracksuit and put it on. Her sports bag was where she had left it the previous week – by the front door. She grabbed her long brown winter coat and opened the door, leaving the lights on.

The weather was fine and clear so Sue decided her grey Astra could stay parked in the road. The ten-minute walk to the Torbay Leisure Centre would do her good she concluded. The cold March wind bit into her face and ruffled her hair but the tracksuit and coat kept her warm as she walked determinedly along the Dartmouth Road. She went past the Big Tree towards the leisure centre situated in the beautiful green lung of Clennon Valley between the densely populated areas of central Paignton and Goodrington. Sue thought about Easter – now only four weeks away. Would she be alone this year or would a rich dark handsome stranger cross her path. She waved to her friend, Sally, as she approached the entrance, and she saw her waiting inside. They liked coming once a week to try and keep fit.

'Hi, Sal, sorry I'm a bit late. Have you been waiting long?'

'No, only a couple of minutes. I got held up in Paignton town centre. The traffic was very bad tonight. I saw you trying to cross Penwill Way.'

'I didn't see you, perhaps I was daydreaming.'

They made their way quickly to the fitness centre.

'Shall we have a drink in the bar afterwards?' suggested Sue as they changed.

'All right but only for a little while. Bill is working late tonight and you know how hopeless he is at getting his own food.' They both laughed.

'How's your sex life?' enquired Sally.

'Non-existent for the last few weeks since I finished with David.'

'You haven't got a new man in your life?'

'Not yet but give me time.'

'With your looks and figure I don't expect you'll be on your own for long.'

Sue smiled. She hoped her friend was right.

Peter was looking forward to his game of squash at the leisure centre. He usually managed to beat Johnny fairly easily but he was good enough to make it competitive for a few minutes until his extra pounds and lack of fitness let him down.

'Look at that torso of yours. There's not an ounce of fat on you. Mandy must be very pleased.' remarked Johnny as they showered afterwards.'

'Let's put it this way, I haven't heard any complaints,' replied Peter, smiling.

Johnny let out a raucous laugh. 'You're keeping her well satisfied, are you, mate? I envy you – she's lovely.'

'Are you having a drink in the bar tonight?' asked Peter.

'Not tonight, Pete, I'm on the early morning shift sorting out all those fucking letters tomorrow. I hate working at the post office – I wish I could get another job. No, you're on your own tonight, mate – don't do anything I wouldn't do.'

'I'll see you next week then,' said Peter as he put on his tie.

'Yes sure, mate. Now that we're alone, can I have a quick word?' Johnny came and sat next to him on the bench. 'You remember those times when I used to get us cannabis?'

'Sure, and the time you got us some crack just to try.'

'What did you think of it?'

'I can take it or leave it.'

'Me too, mate, me too. Well, I've started up a little sideline, just to help a few mates you understand. People get stuffed by the main dealers you know.'

Peter felt a sinking feeling in the pit of his stomach. 'I should be very careful with this, Johnny. Don't give up the day job.'

'You don't understand, Pete, it's just to help a few mates who've asked me. But you know where I am if you need anything.'

'Thanks, Johnny, but count me out.'

Peter sat at the bar contemplating whether to have a second half of lager or make his way home when he noticed Sally sitting at a table in the corner. It must have been three years since he had last seen her. Someone, he couldn't recall who, had told him she was now married. She had been good fun but there had had never been anything serious between them and they had parted as good friends. Her job in an old people's home, working strange hours, had made it difficult as well. *But who*, he wondered, *was that beautiful brunette sitting with her.* He picked up his almost empty glass and walked over to their table to find out.

'Hello, Sally, long time since I've seen you.'

'Hi, Peter, come and sit down.'

He gave her an affectionate kiss on the cheek. 'Is it true you've got married?'

'Yes, I got married a year ago to Bill. I think you met him once, didn't you? It was that time we went out in a group.'

'Yes, I remember Bill – nice guy.' Peter glanced again at the willowy brunette – she was ravishing!

'This is my friend, Sue. We've been coming here for the last six weeks to try and keep fit.'

'It looks as though you're succeeding,' said Peter, noticing that Sue's glass was empty. 'What are you both having to drink?' he asked.

'Nothing for me, Peter, I've got to dash in a minute,' replied Sally.

Sue pushed her glass towards him. 'I'll have another lager and lime please,' she said, smiling at him.

Peter found it difficult not to stare at her. Her short immaculate hair and stunningly beautiful face captivated him. The only blemish was a slightly too large nose but those entrancing large brown eyes, well, they were a knockout!

'Where do you work?' he asked.

'In a photographic shop in Paignton. Most of the time I'm in the shop but sometimes my boss sends me out on assignments. I like that part of my job best.'

'How long have you worked there?'

'Nearly three years. I did think of setting up my own business a year or so ago but decided against it. You need so much capital these days and I like sleeping at night. What do you do?'

'I'm the manager of an insurance agency in Torquay – at the top end in Torre. It's pretty boring at times but we're doing quite well. Do you live in Paignton?'

'Yeah, I've got my own flat, not a million miles away from here.'

'You live on your own then.'

'Yes, all on my own. Not even a cat to keep me warm at night!'

By the time Sue had finished the second drink he had bought her she was giggling a lot and finding it difficult to concentrate. Peter badly needed to visit the gents. All the old demons were back with a vengeance. He really fancied her! Probably, he calculated, she would have her own condoms, but it would be better to be on the safe side. In the toilets he glanced up at the machine and reached into his pocket for some pound coins. He was relieved to find the machine well stocked. It would only be a bit of fun and a one-night stand. Mandy would never find out!

'How did you get here tonight?' enquired Peter.

'I only live about ten minutes' walk away so I walked it.'

'I'll give you a lift home if you like.'

'Thanks, that would be nice.'

They emerged into the bracing night air and made for Peter's car. She grinned at him as he opened the passenger door for her.

As Peter parked his Escort outside Sue's flat he saw a smile appear on her face.

'Would you like to come inside for coffee?'

He did not hesitate. 'That sounds very nice.'

He leant over and kissed her strongly on the lips. She responded by placing her tongue provocatively inside his mouth. He felt his excitement and anticipation increasing rapidly.

The coffee was too strong but he managed to drink half of it. The rest he deposited down the kitchen sink. Sue had disappeared into the bedroom but had thoughtfully put on a romantic cassette. He felt himself becoming aroused and his hand moved towards his crotch. Suddenly the bedroom door opened and he was delighted with the vision before him. All she had on was a pair of tiny white knickers. She smiled at him and moved slowly across the room before finally sitting on his lap. His mouth moved instinctively towards her enticing, neatly rounded breasts and he found her hard left nipple. He sucked enthusiastically as she started to undo his shirt.

'I've left these panties on especially for you to take off,' she cooed tantalisingly into his ear.

He was on fire for her. Soon she stood up – caught hold of his hand and gently lead him into the bedroom. He noticed a packet of condoms lying on top of the bed. She turned to face him, her beautiful body soft and appealing. God, how he wanted to see what was underneath those knickers!

Peter wearily opened his eyes and looked at his watch. It showed ten minutes past seven. He hadn't got much sleep and her sexual appetite had astonished him. He felt shattered but satisfied. She gave a little sigh as if his movement had disturbed her. She slowly opened her eyes and smiled at him, lifting herself up and kissing him on top of his nose.

'You were very good, Peter. I can't remember when I last had so much fun in bed with a man. You seemed to enjoy yourself as well. We must do it again some time.'

Peter felt himself getting hard again. She soon noticed and started to giggle. 'Do you want me to put your cock in my mouth?'

'God, you're so sexy, Sue.'

She opened another condom and put it on quickly before she gave him more pleasure.

'You're quite big, aren't you?' she remarked as she released him.

Peter thought he might have an unfortunate accident. She took pity on him.

'Do you want to shag me again? By the look on your face and the state of your cock I think you probably do.'

She started to giggle again. Peter was in a big hurry. He moved over on top of her and opened her legs and immediately entered her. This time there was no time for any foreplay as his need was too urgent. It took only a few seconds for him to come. Peter now lay drained and exhausted in bed but Sue, to his dismay, wanted to talk.

'Are you married?'

'No, I'm not. Are you?'

'Are you sure you're not married?'

'Of course I'm sure. Don't be silly.'

'Have you got a steady girlfriend?' persisted Sue.

Almost without thinking he found himself lying. 'Not at the moment. How about you?'

'I did until six weeks ago. It lasted nearly a year but I dumped him. He wants me to back to him but there's no chance.'

Peter reflected on this for a few moments. Wild extravagant thoughts were playing tricks with his mind, the night of glorious uninhibited sex uppermost in his thoughts. He threw caution to the wind.

'Shall we go out for the day on Saturday?' He could hardly believe his impulsiveness but he couldn't stop himself. He watched her weighing up the situation.

'Okay, where do you want to take me?'

He thought quickly. It didn't matter as long as it wasn't local. 'Plymouth would be nice.'

'Okay, that suits me. They've got some nice shops. What time will you pick me up?'

'Would ten be a good time or is that too early?'

She smiled at him. 'Make it ten thirty. Luckily I've got this Saturday off but I like to have a lie-in occasionally.'

Peter looked at his watch. He was horrified to see it showed eight fifteen. 'Look at the bloody time, I'll be late for work.'

'Do you want me to make you some breakfast?' asked Sue half-heartedly as she pulled the quilt further up towards her face.

'No time, I'm afraid. I'll get some coffee in the office.' He felt the stubble on his chin. 'First I've got to go home, shave and put a suit on.' He hastily finished dressing. 'I'll leave my phone number on the dressing table.' He wrote it down on a piece of paper. He thought of giving her his card but remembered it had his mobile number on it. She mustn't know that!

'See you on Saturday, Sue.' He walked briskly out of the bedroom, pulling his keys out of his pocket as he went. As he reached the front door he heard her call out to him.

'When you bring me back here on Saturday I might invite you in for a coffee. Would you like that?'

He closed the door quietly behind him without answering.

He started the car and switched on the radio. He could feel his heart racing. His mind was in turmoil. How was he going to resist this sexy girl? *More importantly*, he wondered, *did he want to resist her?* He already knew, beyond any doubt, that this was going to be far more than a one-night stand.

He turned into the main road to Torquay, less than a ten-minute drive away if the traffic was light. Now he was marooned in the rush hour and came to a shuddering halt as the usual traffic congestion took effect. By the time he had cleared the bottleneck at the Preston traffic lights and entered Torquay a daring plan had started to ferment in his mind. He loved Mandy. He adored her. There was no way he could contemplate giving her up. *Perhaps*, he thought, *with a bit of cunning and ingenuity I could have my cake and eat it.*

The quickest way from Paignton to Plymouth, as Peter well knew having lived all his life in Torquay, was via the back roads. First he took the narrow winding road from Paignton to Totnes passing through the picturesque villages of Marldon and Berry Pomeroy and skirting the lovely Westerland Valley. Then into the small quaint medieval town of Totnes crossing the River Dart. Now he took the old B3210 with the beautiful lush green countryside everywhere they looked until they reached the pretty village of Avonwick. A mile further on and Peter gingerly manoeuvred his car on to the busy dual carriageway of the A38. Soon they could see the snow-capped hills and rugged landscape of Dartmoor to the west.

'This could be a day for snowploughs on Dartmoor,' said Peter as he momentarily took his eye off the road.

Soon they glimpsed the outskirts of Plymouth to the east. Now much of the impressive city of over a quarter a million people was spread out in front of them. It was barely thirty minutes since they had set out from Paignton. Peter followed the signs to the city centre.

'I expect you'll want to look round the shops first,' said Peter as he drove along the river embankment towards the seafront and the adjacent city centre. He saw her eyes sparkle with anticipation.

'That sounds a great idea, I need to buy a suit and one or two other things.'

Peter grimaced. She reprimanded him playfully. 'Don't worry if I don't find what I'm looking for very quickly I'll give up.'

'I don't believe a word of it, you women are all the same.' Peter glanced over at her, smiling. She grinned back.

As usual for a Saturday, the popular pedestrianised shopping area of Plymouth was packed. Peter was amazed and delighted that his fears about the suit were not realised as she made a purchase in the second shop they entered. Peter was handed the bag to carry.

'I didn't have time to have any breakfast, I didn't get up early enough,' she informed him as they left the department store.

'I'm feeling a bit peckish now, Peter. Can we have some lunch? I know a nice place just round the next corner.'

'Lead the way.'

The restaurant was already crowded although it was only twelve fifteen. They spotted an empty table and commandeered it quickly. Eventually they got served and had a pleasant two-course meal.

'Have you finished shopping or are there any more things you need to buy?' asked Peter as they drank their coffee. She hesitated and then smiled mischievously at him.

'I think I need to buy some knickers.'

'Well, that shouldn't take very long.'

'Perhaps you can help me choose. After all you may be taking them off later.'

She started to giggle. Peter felt himself blushing hoping that the elderly couple sitting at the next table hadn't heard. *Still*, he thought, *having recovered from the shock, her prediction might turn out to be fairly accurate.* They left quickly. He could see her brief rest had only fortified her for the challenges ahead and the morning shopping had only been a warm-up for the real thing. Not only did she buy some underwear but several other things as well. A pair of trousers, a dress and two jumpers. Peter diligently carried the bags to the car parked a few hundred yards from the Plymouth Pavilions, and placed them in the boot. It was now past three o'clock and they set out on the short walk to the Hoe. The heavy overnight rain had disappeared but as they reached the seafront the wind became much fresher. Luckily they were both wrapped up to resist the icy south-easterly wind blowing in strongly from the sea.

'This gale is ruining my hair,' announced Sue as she fought a valiant but losing battle with the elements.

They looked out over the choppy water. A solitary warship nestled comfortably in the centre of Plymouth Sound, near the breakwater, straight ahead of them. To their right lay the mysterious and forbidding

Drake's Island and behind that the inviting green promise of the Cornish coastline to the west of the River Tamar.

'That island reminds me a bit of Alcatraz,' said Sue.

'Perhaps they could turn it into a prison,' said a surprised Peter.

Sue turned her attention to the warship. 'I really wonder what the point is of this country having all these warships and nuclear submarines,' she announced to an unsuspecting Peter. He stood there flabbergasted.

'You're not a pacifist, are you?'

'No, I'm not, it just seems to me that the whole thing is overkill. When is this country ever going to use a nuclear weapon?'

'That's not the point,' countered Peter. 'The success of having a nuclear deterrent is never having to use it. It's no use this country depending entirely on the Americans. You do realise that thousands of jobs in this city depend on the navy.'

'Yes, I do realise that. Some Plymouth girls married Americans during and after the war. I know of one who went to live in Oregon.'

'Yeah, but more were left pregnant and never saw them again,' replied Peter. 'Let's walk as far as the Barbican.'

They walked along the seafront past the towering lighthouse, situated high up on the Hoe, which had been transported from further along the Cornish coast and was now a tourist attraction. A few minutes walk and they reached the Plymouth Dome – an impressive attractive modern building. They contrasted this with what lay immediately opposite, the poignant neglect of an enormous rotting semicircular swimming pool. Soon the uplifting site of the marina came into view and the large National Marine Aquarium. They walked down to the modern and attractive Barbican shopping centre almost by the water's edge.

Peter was not totally surprised when Sue showed some interest in the shops.

'Peter, I'll just pop into this one if you don't mind, I'll only be a second. Those shoes look really smashing, I need to try them on.'

It was some considerable time before she finished browsing and buying and they started to make their way back to the car.

'Do you pay off your credit cards off every month?' enquired Peter as they eventually got under way.

'No, I don't. I must admit I find it difficult to stop buying things. Anyway it's all your fault for taking me to such a nice place and putting temptation in my way.' She started giggling again.

They stopped at a small café on the way back to the car. This was partly because Sue said she was thirsty and partly to give Peter a rest from all the carrier bags he was now carrying. He sipped his boiling hot tea in silence. He was thinking.

'I don't quite know why I'm carrying four bags to your two,' he finally asked. He was disappointed in her response.

'Because you're a lot stronger than me, Peter.'

He resumed his tea drinking in silence. He was too worn out to complain further.

Sue had been thinking as well. Suddenly she blurted it out, 'Peter, I've been mulling something over in my mind. I usually get alternate Saturdays off. The weekend after next I've got free and I'm planning to visit my parents, brother and sister. I was wondering if you wanted to come.'

He felt intrigued but wary. 'Where do they live?'

'Tavistock.'

Peter felt his heartbeat increasing. This was ideal. They lived miles away – right across the other side of Devon.

'That sounds great – I'd love to come.'

Peter had regained his strength and they started off again. He felt more relaxed and the bags appeared lighter.

'We should have taken a taxi back with all those bags,' said Sue as they reached the car.

'Nonsense, it was great to get some fresh air,' replied Peter as he opened the car door.

They stopped for a meal in a pub in Totnes. Peter felt nervous as it was too close to home for comfort. As he sat down away from the bar he thought he saw somebody he recognised. Instinctively he turned his head away and tried to shield his face with his hand. He felt himself getting hot and bothered. *Was this*, he wondered, *the way life was going to be in the future. Perhaps it was, but it was worth the danger.* He glanced up again and the person he recognised seemed to have gone. Very soon they would be back in the safety of her flat. The excitement of another night with Sue beckoned.

'Let's take a shower together,' suggested Sue as they relaxed with cold beers from the fridge. Peter needed no second invitation as he quickly finished his drink. They left their clothes on the living room floor and stepped into the shower cubicle. Sue giggled as the warm water cascaded down on them and their bodies touched in the confined space.

'My word, Peter, you are getting excited!' she purred as she saw his erection and gave him a playful tug.

Peter immediately responded by pulling her close to him, squeezing her breasts and kissing her strongly on the mouth. He found her irresistible. After they dried each other in the living room, he carried her into the bedroom and she gave him oral sex. She liked doing it. He liked receiving it. Soon they scrambled underneath the sheets and Peter got to work as he already knew what she liked. Urgently she pulled his head down between her legs and he instantly found the sweet spot amongst her thick dark pubic hair. He licked her with the tip of his tongue and then pushed the end down harder. She let out a soft moan of pleasure. He pulled away and kissed her belly button.

'Don't stop, you bastard – finish me off,' she pleaded.

He kissed her on the mouth, teasing her for a brief moment, and she pulled her mouth away. He smiled at her. He knew exactly where she wanted to be kissed. She pushed his head down between her legs again.

'Please don't stop, Peter.'

He did not let her down. Soon she exploded loudly with pleasure and relief. He buried his head in her breasts, as she lay back satisfied.

'You're very wet, did you enjoy that?' he asked unnecessarily. She quickly regained her composure.

'Now it's your turn to have some fun,' she declared as she grabbed hold of him and guided him in between her legs. Peter was ready and eager. This time they both came quickly and together.

Much later, after Sue had fallen contentedly asleep, he lay awake thinking. The sex was fantastic! It was the best he had ever experienced and the physical attraction was immense. It wasn't his fault that she was too sexy to resist. In two weeks they would be off to Tavistock – the other side of Dartmoor. He already knew he was looking forward to going.

His thoughts turned to tomorrow. He was taking Mandy to Totnes to see his mother and aunt. Now that his sexual appetite had been satisfied, at least for the moment, he suddenly found himself consumed with guilt and tenderness towards the lovely girl he was going to marry. He wanted to see her now. He wanted to kiss her and tell her he loved her and missed her. He wanted to tell her that he was sorry and that the attraction was purely sexual. He looked at the beautiful temptress lying beside him. Could he resist her? Could he walk away now and concentrate on the girl he loved more than anything in the world? He knew the answer. It was an emphatic – no!

Peter woke late on Sunday morning. He was amazed to smell the distinctive aroma of bacon frying. Sue had clearly surpassed herself. He jumped expectantly out of bed and got dressed.

'This is a nice surprise,' said Peter as he parked himself on a chair and waited.

'Oh you're up. That's good, I was about to come and wake you.'

'I can't believe you've done this.'

'I can do it when I try. Do you want one egg or two?'

'Two, I think, I'm starving.'

Within a couple of minutes she was ready to serve. He polished it all off in double quick time. He looked at his watch. It was almost time to pick up Mandy.

'I've got to go and see my mother later on, Sue, so I've got to dash. Shall I come round in the week?'

'Wednesday would be a good day, Peter.'

'Yeah, Wednesday suits me as well. I'll be over at about seven. Some evenings I have to work late,' he lied. He gave her a brief kiss on the lips and left. He was anxious not to be late picking up Mandy.

Sue was more than happy for Peter to take his car for the journey to Tavistock. He decided to take the scenic route across Dartmoor. The early morning spring sunshine indicated a pleasant day ahead.

'I promise not to buy any clothes this afternoon,' said Sue as they left Paignton town centre.

Peter failed to suppress a loud laugh. 'You must have bought enough clothes in Plymouth to last six months.'

'Hardly but I'm running up hefty bills on my cards and I need to get them down. Also there's the rent on the flat that's £250 a month. Then there's the car and the price of petrol. I never seem to save any money.'

'Well, having been shopping in Plymouth with you I can understand that.'

'I'm not always such a spendthrift as that. Sometimes I can be quite responsible.'

They got through the potential bottleneck of Totnes without any problems. Dartmoor was only a few minutes away.

'We can come back on the main roads if you like,' said Peter.

They left the A38 at Ashburton and immediately crossed the Dartmoor National Park boundary. A few miles on they went through the tiny village of Poundsgate. The road was now narrow and tortuous as it rose steeply to the high moorland. Then a swift descent to a more fertile valley with a hotel, a river and a restaurant. But everywhere, across almost the entire moor was a barren landscape of austere rugged emptiness and isolation. There was only the occasional farmhouse, most of which were still occupied, testament that a few hardy souls were still prepared to eke out a precarious living in the unrelenting harsh environment.

'I hardly ever drive across the moor,' said Sue. 'I suppose it's the vastness and unspoilt environment that attracts so many people, but it gives me the shivers. Fancy living here – it would drive me mad.'

Peter knew he did not share her views but nevertheless understood them. 'It's quicker to go on the main roads to Tavistock anyway and miss the moor completely,' he said.

'I'd like you to make a little detour in a minute, Peter. I've got my camera and I want to take some pictures of the prison. It's only a minute or two out of our way.'

Peter hated the dark dingy prison, a blight on the entire moor he reckoned, but they had plenty of time. The road now straightened and Peter speeded up as they passed through the centre of the moor. The small detour hardly cost them any time at all. Sue pointed her camera at Dartmoor Prison and clicked away for a couple of minutes. Despite the stillness and clear visibility it still looked grey, sinister and depressing.

'This is the place that sends shivers down my spine,' said Peter, anxious to make a quick getaway.

'I think I've got enough now. Let's get out of here – this place is horrible, Peter.'

Soon after, they passed through the dull village of Princetown before rejoining the road to Tavistock a few miles further on.

'The area round the prison has four times the average rainfall we get in Torbay – about one hundred inches,' remarked Peter.

'I didn't know that. What a mine of information you are. It sounds as though you need to own an umbrella if you live around here. Mind you, we used to get a fair bit of rain in Tavistock as well.'

He heard that familiar giggle again. He wanted more information about her family. 'Are your brother and sister younger than you?' he asked.

'Yes, Patrick's twenty-five. He works in an estate agency in Plymouth. He got engaged to a nurse last autumn and she lives with her parents in Plymouth. Jo is much younger and still at school. She's just about to take her A levels. She's a bright kid so she should do well.'

'When did you say your father retired?'

'Last summer. He had a heart bypass two years ago and he's got back trouble. The teaching job was getting too much for him anyway. He took early retirement at fifty-two.'

'Will your mother keep on working?'

'I think so. She only works part-time as a nurse in a doctor's surgery in Tavistock. Turn next left, we're almost there.'

Peter noticed straight away that Sue's father didn't look well but he decided not to say anything to Sue. Her mother was friendly but looked harassed. Jo had the same trim figure as her much older sister without the same stunning beauty and she was shy. *What a contrast to her sister*, thought Peter. Her brother arrived in his car after a few minutes. He was good-looking, articulate and oozed confidence. Was it his imagination, Peter wondered, or was Patrick a little cool towards him.

After lunch Sue was very keen to show Peter round the town she was brought up in. They followed the path of the River Tavy through the small town.

'Some of these buildings are very attractive,' said Peter as they reached the main shopping area.

'I deliberately left my credit cards behind to avoid temptation,' she announced as they glanced at some ladies' clothes in a shop window.

'That was very wise after your binge in Plymouth. I need a pair of trousers so you'll just have to watch me this week.' Despite trying on several pairs he failed to find what he was looking for.

'I suppose I could always borrow your card if I find something I can't do without,' said Sue, her resolve starting to weaken. To Peter's relief this proved to be unnecessary.

'Why did you move to Torbay?' asked Peter as they walked hand in hand back to the house.

'I prefer living in urban areas to the countryside, Tavistock is a nice friendly town but it wasn't big enough for me. I didn't want to move out of Devon so when I saw this photographic job advertised in Paignton I jumped at it. I remember I wore my shortest skirt to the interview. Perhaps that helped me get the job!' she added, laughing.

As the house was full their lovemaking was restrained and inhibited. Peter wondered how many other men she had invited to her parents' house. He was concerned about something else which he mentioned as they lay together in bed.

'I got the impression that your brother is a bit suspicious of me.'

'Really, you do surprise me. It's probably because he got on so well with David.'

'Did he come here often?'

'Several times. We did go out for a year, you know.'

'Yeah, so you said. Why did you finish with him?'

'He got too possessive. He wanted us to get married but I said no. Then a few weeks later I ended it. I just...' her voice tailed off as she searched for the right words. 'I just got tired of him, I guess. I'm sure I did the right thing.'

Peter changed the subject. 'Are you sure you don't want to go back across the moor?'

'Not bloody likely! The place gives me the creeps.'

'Okay, then we'll stick to our original plan.'

'Can I stay at your house tomorrow night?'

Alarm bells started to ring in his head. The neighbours might see! Already he had taken some elaborate precautions. She still did not know he had a mobile phone and he had left that at home as usual. If headquarters wanted to contact him urgently that was too bad, they could always leave a message. He quickly gathered his thoughts.

'The house will be freezing, I left the central heating off.' He was relieved to see her relent. Luckily she hated the cold.

Peter had not enjoyed the weekend as much as he'd hoped. He felt his thoughts wander as he drove into Plymouth on the A386, past the airport. They didn't have a lot in common; it was basically physical attraction and sex. He knew it was dangerous and he was playing with fire. She was intelligent and fun to be with, not like Mandy, of course, but nobody could measure up to her. Within an hour they would be back in Sue's flat. This time his suit would be hanging in Sue's wardrobe. Another night of lust and pleasure was certain. If it weren't for the subterfuge everything in the garden would be rosy.

Chapter Five

Sue walked out into the warm late-June sunshine and gathered her thoughts. There was no time to walk as it was almost six already and she was due to meet Sally at the leisure centre on the hour. She needed to get back afterwards quickly because Peter had said he was coming over at eight. Sue also wanted a chance to talk to Sally in the café area when they had finished their workout. She started the car quickly. It would only take a couple of minutes to get there. Why Peter had stopped meeting her at the leisure centre on Tuesdays was a mystery to her. All he ever seemed to want to do was stay in her flat and when he did take her out it usually entailed going to Exeter, Plymouth or Totnes. It was true he was taking her to Brixham on Friday but she had had to badger him into that. She parked the car in the leisure centre car park and hastily made her way to the entrance.

'How long is it since you started going out with Peter?' asked Sally as they relaxed in the café after a strenuous session on the machines.

'Over three months.'

'Are you keen this time? You look very happy and your complexion is super. Is he still as good in bed?'

Sue thought she detected a note of envy in her friend's voice. She felt the need to rub it in.

'No problem on that score, I can assure you. The sex is great.'

'Perhaps this time it will turn into something permanent, with a ring on your finger.'

'I'm not very keen on wearing rings, Sal. However it might be time for me to think of settling down with a man. I am twenty-seven after all.'

'Somehow I can't really see you with a bevy of kids in tow,' said Sally as she offered Sue a digestive biscuit.

'You're right there. If he wants any kids he'll just have to wait. I don't want any – not for at least five years anyway. What about you?'

Sally grinned back at her. 'We're trying at the moment. Bill's a bit of a dunce in bed but he's probably capable of making me pregnant. I certainly hope so at any rate.' They both laughed loudly.

'Peter's got a good job, perhaps he's ready to take the plunge,' said Sally.

'Perhaps he is – and he's got his own house as well. The job is quite well paid and I earn good money. Together we probably bring in over £35,000 a year and that's a lot for Torbay. Perhaps he'll ask me soon, Sal. And if he does, you never know, I might say yes! Goodness, is that the time? I need to get back to the flat. See you next week, Sal.'

Peter made some coffee in Sue's flat. He was ten minutes early so he was not surprised to find that she had not arrived back. The flat, he observed, was immaculate as usual. Heaven help him if he had the audacity to make a mess. The fish and chips, which he had bought on the way, were reheating in the oven, the oily paper, as instructed, neatly deposited in the waste bin. He looked at his watch and saw it was past her promised arrival time. He went to the window just in time to see her parking the car, squeezing it delicately into a small space directly outside the flat. He blew a kiss to her as she emerged smiling.

'Hi, Peter, I'm absolutely famished. That smell is making me even more hungry. Did you get me some plaice?'

'I did indeed.'

She rushed towards him and planted a long kiss on his mouth. 'I've not seen you for five days. I've missed you.'

'I've been very busy at work, Sue. You know I have to work late several nights a week.'

She broke away from his arms. 'That's just a little something to be getting on with,' she teased as she went into the kitchen to fetch some plates, knives and forks.

Peter had already made himself useful by putting the bread, butter and lemon juice on the table. The electric kettle boiled and switched itself off.

'Do you want to eat in front of the telly or in here?' asked Sue.

'In here, there's only rubbish on.'

'Be a pet and get the milk out of the fridge, Peter, please.'

He obliged. They had nearly finished the meal when her growing frustration came to the surface.

'Can we go to the multiplex in Paignton next week?'

Peter felt himself tense. He paused for a moment. 'I'd rather go to the one in Plymouth, it's twice the size and I like the restaurant better.'

'Why is it that we never go anywhere in Paignton or Torquay?'

'Well, we're in the holiday season now. Everywhere gets so crowded during the summer in Torbay. Besides I get bored going to all the same old places I've known all my life.' He glanced at her, hoping like mad that he was sounding convincing.

She did not respond at once, preferring to pour herself another cup of tea. Finally, she spoke. 'Okay, then let's go to the multiplex in Plymouth but only on condition that I choose the film.'

Peter felt himself relax. The danger was over, at least for the moment. Peter knew he would need to tell her at some stage. He had thought this through interminably and had come to the conclusion that the time to do it was when he came back from his honeymoon. She would be hopping mad, of course, but he would be able to talk her round. After all she enjoyed the sex as much as he did and she didn't want to get married or anything like that. Yes, he was sure he would be able to talk her round. The sex was even better now that she had gone on the pill. No more endless fiddling with those wretched condoms.

Sue searched round the freezer and finally located the chocolate ice cream. There was only enough for two small portions. She gave Peter the slightly smaller one.

'Jo will be coming to stay with me for a couple of weeks when she breaks up,' announced Sue as she cleared away the dishes. 'I'll need to buy a few things for the spare room before she arrives.'

Peter felt comfortable about Jo coming. There was less chance of a problem, he reasoned, if he was seen out in Torbay with two young women. Sue quickly detailed Peter to do the washing-up. This was his usual chore – relatively easy that night as no cooking had been required.

'Do you want a lager?' asked Sue as she studied the contents of her fridge.

'What else have you got?'

'Nothing much. It looks like it's that or nothing,' added Sue apologetically as she found the cupboard nearly bare. 'Do you want the lager?'

'Yes please – that's fine.'

'I'll have to go to Sainsbury's tomorrow and get in more supplies. I can't understand how I've got so low. It must be that I've got a lot on my mind at the moment, Peter.' She passed him a mug of coffee and they adjourned to the living room settee to watch the news headlines.

As usual they were soon in bed. Their passion still as ardent and intense as it was when they had first met. Their desire to explore each other's bodies and give one another pleasure still paramount in their lovemaking. The mutual attraction showed no sign of abating. Neither thought they were in love but the physical desires, if anything, were becoming stronger and intensifying. The very dangerous liaison still shone brightly and refused to die.

Chapter Six

Zoe, of course, had been pencilled in as a bridesmaid right from the start. Heaven help anyone who had the temerity to suggest otherwise. She was a trump card that had to be played early and boldly. Peter was designated the job of finding a suitable location for a memorable honeymoon and he was happy with this assignment.

Peter was more than happy to leave the intricacies of wedding dresses, wedding invitations, wedding presents and wedding receptions to Mandy and her mother. In fact he was only too happy to keep out of her mother's way as much as possible. He was more convinced than ever that she hated him. He was certain she must have tried to persuade Mandy to look elsewhere for a partner. But he was going to have the last laugh as Mandy was steadfast in her love for him. Still they seemed to be doing quite well with the complicated arrangements. They had chosen a day – Saturday 6 October – a church and a hotel for the reception. It was a big hotel as well, close to Livermead Sands, overlooking the sea.

'Will you be my best man?' Peter had asked Jim way back in April.

'Of course I will, thanks for asking me. You can rely on me to make a good speech and keep you out of mischief.'

Peter laughed. 'You didn't keep me out of mischief at the party, did you? Who kept filling my glass with champagne?'

'I didn't know you had drunk all that lager,' replied Jim innocently.

'Never again will I mix lager and champagne.'

'Are you going to have a stag night?'

'After what happened at the party I think I'll try to avoid that.'

'Well, if you change your mind I'm willing.'

'I doubt I will. Just make sure I don't make a fool of myself at the wedding.'

Peter wanted to make the honeymoon special. He wracked his brain hoping for some inspiration. He asked his colleagues at work. He read the quality newspapers. He browsed in all the travel agents and took away their brochures. He wanted somewhere steaming hot and exotic. Finally he came up with the answer.

'Would you like to go to Acapulco for our honeymoon?'

'Where's that, Peter? I told you geography was not my strong subject.'

He produced a map. 'See, it's on the Pacific coast of Mexico. I've made enquiries at the travel agents. We could fly to the capital, Mexico City, spend a day or two there and then travel to Acapulco by coach. Stay there for a week and then take another coach back to Mexico City. The cost is much cheaper than I thought.'

'Is it hot?'

'Boiling, but apparently all the hotels have air conditioning. The beaches are supposed to be wonderful. Well, you can see from the pictures in this brochure I got. We're bound to get a suntan.'

She looked quickly at the brochure and smiled at him. 'Where do we fly from?'

'Heathrow, direct to Mexico City with British Airways. The flight takes about eleven hours.'

'I like flying British Airways. It sounds exciting, Peter, let's go there.'

Peter, now feeling pleased with himself, changed the subject. 'I hope you and your mum aren't inviting too many people to the wedding.'

'I thought about seventy.'

'We should end up with lots of presents with that number.'

'We've arranged to have a presents' list printed, Peter. If we ask less than seventy some people are going to be disappointed.'

He moved over and gave her a soft kiss on the cheek. 'Carry on the good work, darling – don't let me interfere.'

Mandy's mood varied as the big day loomed ever closer. Most of the time she oozed happiness. But sometimes Peter could feel her nervous tension as she agonised over whether everything would be all right on the day. He tried to allay her fears but her sad days made him nervous and anxious.

'I wish it was all over and we were on our honeymoon,' she confided in him as the countdown reached the last few weeks. 'I'm getting so nervous and I love you so much, Peter. I don't want to let you down. You've been working so hard at work during the last few months as well. I don't see half as much of you as I used to.'

Peter put his arm round her and gave her a reassuring squeeze. 'What are you talking about, Mandy? I'm the lucky one marrying such a wonderful person as you. I know I've been busy at work but it's all in aid of our future.'

'Yes, I know that. I don't know why I get down so easily.'

'Everything is going to be fine at the wedding and it's going to be a great day. Almost everyone we've invited is coming. Don't worry.'

He looked intently into her face. It broke into that delightful smile that still sent his heart pounding with love and desire for her. He knew, without question, that he was the luckiest man alive to be marrying Mandy.

Peter was glad it wasn't going to be a posh wedding. The idea, introduced by his future mother-in-law, that he should wear a morning suit had thankfully been ruled out.

'Your father wore one at our wedding,' he heard her say to Mandy.

'But Peter wouldn't feel comfortable in it, Mum,' said Mandy taking his side.

'Well, if the silly man won't wear one then we'll have to make the best of a bad job.'

Peter could have strangled her but as he had won the argument he decided to keep quiet. Now he gazed into the mirror and admired his new lounge suit. What on earth was she complaining about? The suit fitted perfectly. The carnation would go well with it. In three weeks they would be married and his happiness would be complete.

His thoughts turned briefly to Sue. She had been surprised when he had told her he was going to Mexico for a two-week holiday with friends. In fact she seemed a little bit cross.

'It was booked months ago, before I met you.'

'Why didn't you tell me before, I might have wanted to come.'

'I just forgot,' he replied lamely. He felt very uncomfortable. Should he have risked a blazing row and told her the unpalatable truth. He had decided against it as the consequences of telling her were predictable. He had wisely opted for caution; the time to tell her was when he came back from the honeymoon. Unquestionably he had definitely made the right decision.

Saturday 6 October was a perfect early autumn day. The cloudless sky and high temperatures were more in keeping with high summer as

Torbay basked in the perfect weather. The sea was clear and inviting as a gentle south-westerly breeze broke the stillness hanging over the resort. By mid-morning, several small sailing craft had ventured out into the bay to take advantage of the ideal conditions.

It was also the day that Peter John Carpenter and Amanda Teresa Wyatt were due to get married at Central Church, Torquay at two o'clock. Peter had woken up after a restless night feeling more nervous than he had anticipated. He managed to force down some breakfast – two Weetabix followed by a small piece of wholemeal toast, washed down with orange juice. Now it was time to phone Mandy to see if she was as panic-stricken as he was. He picked up his mobile phone and dialled. To his dismay her mother answered. He had hoped for a warmer reception.

'What do you want, Peter?' she barked frostily.

'I wanted to speak to Mandy.'

'She can't speak to you now, she's in the middle of having her hair done.'

'How long will that take?'

'Not too long, I hope. She's got lot's of other things to do.'

'I'll phone in about half an hour.'

'If you must but it's a bit chaotic here and we're going to be very busy. I wish you were wearing the morning suit, Peter. Mandy is going to be looking so lovely in her wedding dress. You are going to be looking your best this afternoon, aren't you?'

Peter felt himself getting hot under the collar. 'Not really, I was thinking of coming along in my slippers and an open-necked shirt.'

'Peter, there's no need to be sarcastic.'

He heard Mandy's voice in the background.

'Mum, please give me the phone.'

As usual, he thought, *she came to the rescue.*

'Hello, darling. Did you sleep well last night?' she asked.

'Not really. How about you?'

'I think I slept for about two hours. I was too nervous and excited. Is everything all right at your end?'

'Yeah, my mother is here. So are Jane, Steve and the kids. They'll be bringing Zoe over in about half an hour. She's very excited. My father's going straight to the church for obvious reasons. Jim and Kay should be arriving any minute. What a palaver! We should have got married at the registry office with two witnesses.' He heard her laugh.

'The weather is fantastic, Peter. Aren't we lucky?'

'It looks great at the moment. Don't keep me waiting at the church too long, will you?' he added.

'I'll try not to. I must go, Peter. My hair is not finished yet. See you in church!'

Peter switched his phone off and saw Jim and Kay coming in through the door.

'Peter, you have got the wedding ring, haven't you?' asked Jim frantically.

Peter fumbled nervously in his pockets. Eventually to everyone's relief a box finally emerged. He handed it to Jim. He checked that the ring was actually in the box. Mercifully it was.

Zoe looked as pretty as a picture and she was keen to show off her new hairstyle to anyone who could spare a moment. Her sparkling eyes, pretty face and long blonde hair making it certain, Peter surmised, that after Mandy she would be the star of the show. Kay had taken a liking to Zoe as well.

'What are you looking forward to most at the wedding, Zoe?' she asked.

By the expression on her face Peter could see that Zoe was taking this question seriously.

'The kissing and the trifle and cake.'

'I can probably manage the kissing but the way I'm feeling at the moment I'm not so sure about the trifle and cake,' said Peter, feeling the tension ease slightly as the others laughed.

'Mummy, is it time to go yet?' asked Zoe.

'Yes, it's almost time for us to go,' replied Jane.

'Come on then – everybody in the car,' said Steve.

Soon the car sped away leaving Peter, Jim, Kay and Peter's mother, Josie, behind.

'Your niece is very cute,' said Jim.

'You wait till you see her in the dress. She's looking forward to wearing that,' said Peter proudly.

'It's time for us to go, Peter. You've only got a few minutes of freedom left. There's still time to change your mind,' said Jim, grinning at him.

Peter took a quick drink of water to ease the dryness. 'Let's go, Jim, we don't want to be late.'

The relatively new modern Central Church in the heart of Torquay was only a few minutes' drive away. Jim had deliberately set off a little before time in case of heavy Saturday traffic.

'You're staying the night here, aren't you?' asked Kay.

'Yeah, the plane is due to leave at three in the afternoon so we won't have to set off until nine. It goes direct to Mexico City.'

The sky was now clouding over a little as they embarked from the car. Mandy, Peter knew, would be looking gorgeous. He hoped she wouldn't be too late.

The church was warm and welcoming. Peter smiled nervously as he waited. Jim had the ring and he was going to pass it to him at the appropriate moment – unless he dropped it on the floor. The vicar smiled at him and he smiled back. He kept looking at his watch incessantly. Where on earth was she? Perhaps they'd had an accident!

Then to his relief the music started. It took an age for her to join him at the altar. He did not look at her until she was almost alongside him. He lifted his gaze and their eyes met. Her face broke into a beaming loving smile. She looked stunning. He felt the nerves and tension melt away. This was the moment he had been waiting for. Mandy, the girl of his dreams, was going to marry him. He knew he could make her very happy. He was certain this was the best day of his life!

Chapter Seven

Sue still felt a tiny bit envious. She was certain she could have done with two weeks' sunbathing on an exotic Mexican beach. She wondered who these friends were that he was going with. She certainly hadn't met any of them. She wouldn't be seeing him for over two weeks. It would be sensible, she reasoned, that as this was her weekend off it would be best to go back home for the weekend rather than moping around her flat. She needed sympathy. She rang her mother.

'He's gone off to Mexico for two weeks and left me here, Mum. I feel a bit down so can I come home for the weekend? I can take Monday off as well as I've still got a day's holiday to use up.'

'Of course, darling. Come home any time you want. It will be lovely to see you.'

Sue put the phone down feeling a little better. At least somebody loved her and wanted to see her – even if it was only her mum. She'd much rather be flying to the tropical paradise that Peter and his friends were destined to arrive at shortly but nevertheless she would have to make the best of a bad situation. *He'd better bring me back a nice present*, she thought.

To keep her mind occupied she decided to start packing her overnight bag. She had almost finished when the telephone rang. Surprisingly it was her boss, Philip. He sounded decidedly croaky.

'I think I must have got flu,' he spluttered. 'Can you do a job for me tomorrow? I feel dreadful. I think I need to spend tomorrow in bed.'

Sue felt sympathetic. Philip always treated her fairly.

'Well, I was going home to see my family this weekend but I can leave it for a week or two if you need me.'

'I'd be grateful if you would.'

'Okay, I'll do it. What's the job?'

There was a short pause while Philip cleared his throat. 'The usual thing on a Saturday afternoon – wedding photographs. You need to be at the bride's house at one. The wedding is at the Central Church at two.'

'I might have guessed it would be boring old wedding snaps, Philip. Hang on a minute while I try to find a pen.' Finally she found one. 'Right Philip, what's the bride's address?'

'It's 80 Langridge Terrace, Torquay.'

'Good – I know where that is. It's a nice area. Who are the lucky couple?'

'Amanda Wyatt and Peter Carpenter.'

She froze.

'Are you still there, Sue?'

Somehow she stammered out a reply. 'Can you... can you repeat that?'

'It's Amanda Wyatt and Peter Carpenter.'

She felt as if a stake had been driven through her heart. All she could think about was getting off the phone as soon as possible. She could feel her whole body trembling.

'Okay, Philip, leave it all to me. I hope... I hope you soon get better.'

'Thanks, Sue, you're a real trooper.'

Sue threw herself on the bed crying uncontrollably. Her tears flooded over the pillow. She didn't know how long she stayed there before, somehow, she found the strength to drag herself upright. The telephone rang but she refused to answer it. Her misery overwhelmed her as the tears refused to stop. Without thinking, she took off all her clothes and put on her nightdress. She clambered into bed and the tears flowed freely again. She felt numb in her mind and body. She was in total shock!

She remembered the last time she had seen him – only two days before. He hadn't stayed the night but they had made love for an hour in bed. He had told that her he would phone her from Mexico. He said he would phone her as soon as he got back from his holiday. She remembered the affectionate kiss he had given her as he said goodnight.

'See you soon' were his last words as he left her naked in bed. The tears started again as she buried her face in the pillow. She couldn't get his face out of her mind. Why had he done this to her? She kept asking herself the same question over and over again until she thought her mind would explode.

Sleep was impossible. She turned things over in her tortured mind time and time again as she searched vainly for an explanation and tried to come to terms with the shock. How had she allowed herself to be deceived for so long? By the early hours nervous exhaustion allowed her to sleep at last. She woke a few hours later feeling miserable and drained. Her watch showed six thirty. It was still very dark outside.

She dragged herself out of bed and switched on the light. She felt terribly thirsty. The water revived her temporarily and she steeled herself to walk into the bathroom and look at herself in the mirror. She let out an expletive as she saw how ghastly she looked. Her eyes were sore and red. She needed a long shower. The warm, soapy water made her feel almost human again as she let the water run for what seemed like an eternity – trying to wash her unhappiness away. It was working! Her mood was slowly but surely changing from shock and hurt to anger. She could feel the anger and resentment building up inside her as she dried herself and got dressed. Suddenly she felt the urgent need to get out of the flat. There was no time to dry her hair. She needed some fresh air immediately!

The sun was rising out of a cloudless sky as she opened her front door. She rubbed her eyes as the brightness made them hurt. Luckily there was nobody about. She didn't want any of the neighbours to see that she had been crying. At last, now that she was in the open air and away from the claustrophobic flat, she could think straight. Her mood had changed dramatically now that the initial shock was starting to wear off, her anger and thoughts of revenge growing remorselessly within her. The bastard! He was going to pay for what he had done to her!

She took the path alongside the railway line, where the popular steam trains, full of eager holidaymakers would later in the day be disgorging thick black smoke into the sky as they made their way to Kingswear and back. Sue walked briskly into Youngs Park Road with the pretty park on her right. Already the swans and ducks were swimming and feeding in the boating lake. A solitary walker, exercising his dog, crossed the park but Sue, her mind fully engaged elsewhere, was oblivious to him. She marched purposefully on towards Goodrington North beach where only a few weeks before the smooth sands had been packed with excited holidaymakers. Now, as the season reached its end all that was left was a beach caked with thick slimy seaweed brought in by the early morning tide. She continued her walk on past the Whitbread family pub and the impressive water park with its labyrinth of water slides designed for summer fun.

She needed time and space. The beauty of the surroundings at that moment were meaningless to her. Now she walked parallel to Goodrington South beach with the beach huts still in position, awaiting transportation to their winter quarters. Hardly a soul was about as she came to the end of the beach and turned into Cliff Park Road and went as far as the new luxury residential flats and the permanently closed chalet holiday complex – both clear signs of the slowly changing, declining holiday industry. Now Sue took the rising coastal footpath climbing high above the bay. Near the top, momentarily she stopped and looked back at the splendour behind her. The blue water glistened far below as she looked over the sea to Torquay. She pressed on a little further until she turned off to return to the main Dartmouth Road. She walked back past the Three Beaches shops with the enormous sprawling Waterside pub to her left and the charming Dainton Hotel further on to her right. She spotted a break in the busy traffic and crossed the road and almost immediately reached the YMCA building. Soon she would be back to the leisure centre and almost home.

By the time she reached her front door she had made up her mind about two things Firstly, nothing on earth was going to stop her taking the wedding photographs. The look on his face when she confronted him, she imagined, would be a sight not to be missed. Secondly, she would never sleep with him again. He had betrayed her and he was going to marry someone else. Amazingly, she had been completely deceived. She reached her flat, feeling exhausted but better. The long walk had done her a power of good.

She opened her fridge and fished out a fresh carton of orange juice. Sue had no stomach for any food but the sharp taste of the juice tasted good. She poured out a second glass and went and sat down in the living room. What a stupid fool she had been! The reason for his evasiveness was now abundantly clear. She felt deep pain inside her. But it was now the pain of anger, almost hatred, towards the man who had deceived her. She was now thirsty for revenge!

She lifted her aching limbs out of the armchair and walked towards the bathroom. She wanted to look again in the mirror. Did she still look such a hideous sight? She was relieved at what greeted her. *With some make-up*, she thought, *I can make myself presentable.* The tears had gone now, at least for the time being, and she felt able to cope. But it was unquestionably the fact that she had been duped that rankled the most. How could he have betrayed her like that? She searched in vain for an answer.

The time until one o'clock passed so slowly. Sue started to wonder what this young woman was like. She couldn't know about her – that much was certain. She was sure to be pretty. Soon she would be able to see for herself. She didn't want to arrive before one. The suspense was killing her as she fiddled with her radio to try and pass the time. When that became tiresome and boring she resorted to playing a cassette. One question kept repeating itself to her. If it hadn't been for Philip's flu she would still be ignorant of what was about to happen. How long had he expected to get away with it?

The house stood well back from the road. It was obviously an affluent area with well-manicured gardens and attractive detached houses in the tree-lined street. She glanced up at the imposing large house and looked for a parking space. She found one and got out to open the boot. The radiant bride was already walking towards her car.

'Hello, I'm Amanda.'

Sue was initially taken aback. The girl was even more lovely than she had imagined.

'Hello, Amanda, I'm Sue. We need to take several shots of you on your own first.'

Zoe, who had her hands round Mandy's leg, listened intently and started to cry.

'Don't worry, sweetheart, Sue will take some of you in a minute.'

'It's a wonderful day for you to get married,' said Sue as she completed the first shots.

'I know. I'm really thrilled with it. We both are.'

'Have you known your husband for a long time?'

'It was a year ago when we first met. We're both very happy.'

'Come on, Zoe, it's your turn now,' said Sue.

Then it was time for Jason and Zoe to be done together and finally the whole group including Mandy's parents.

Sue waited in the car and caught a glimpse of Peter entering the church. She had made sure that she was too far away for him to see her. Mandy could have him as far as she was concerned. Now it was time for her to get into position as she needed to take some shots of

Mandy and her father entering the church. She managed to stop the sniffles by blowing hard into a paper handkerchief. Now she was ready to go. She wanted Peter to get the shock of his life!

Mandy and her father had entered the church and Sue looked up again at the sky. There were a few puffy white clouds, which obscured the sun from time to time. *Ideal weather*, Sue thought, *for taking wedding photographs*. She allowed herself a thin, wry smile. After all she did want to make these photographs as nice as possible – didn't she? She was now ready and waiting, albeit a little nervously. All she needed now was a bride and, perhaps more importantly, a bridegroom.

Nobody had fluffed their lines. The beautiful ring was safely installed on Mandy's finger. The book had been signed and he had kissed her nicely, full on the lips. Peter was relieved that the difficult part was over. Now it was a question of letting everyone take as many photographs as they wanted and then going off to the hotel. Mandy was exuberant.

'I feel so happy, Peter.'

He gave her another long, lingering kiss. Zoe adjusted Mandy's long wedding dress train and then stood back to admire her handiwork. Mandy put her arm inside Peter's and they started the long walk down the aisle. The bright autumn sunshine embraced them as they emerged into the sunlight, happy and smiling. A few passers-by had stopped to catch a glimpse of the radiant bride. Peter felt so proud as he put his arm round Mandy's slim shoulders. Then, to his horror, he saw Sue's grim, unsmiling face staring coldly at him only a few feet away. His heart started to pump wildly and he felt his legs turn to jelly.

'I'm here to take the official photographs of your wedding, Mr Carpenter,' she said softly, without the hint of a smile. 'I've got another engagement so can we get down to business as soon as possible.'

Peter was dumbstruck. Never in his worst nightmare had he expected anything as horrendous as this. His world had disintegrated. A wooden smile was all he could muster as she painstakingly took more and more photos.

'This is the happiest day of your life, Mr Carpenter. Could you try and smile a bit more and look as though you're enjoying yourself.'

Peter wanted the ground to open up in front of him and make him disappear for ever.

'I need to take some pictures of you and your best man. Where is he?'

Eventually his ordeal was over. 'Enjoy your honeymoon,' was the last thing he heard her say as she went to pack her equipment away.

'Is everything all right, darling? You seem to have gone bit quiet,' asked Mandy as they were being driven to the hotel.

'Yes, everything's fine,' he lied. He found he couldn't look at her. His mind felt like a vacuum. A nightmare scenario loomed in front of him. At least she hadn't made a scene at the church, but he knew that was a small consolation. The look of hatred and contempt on her face, he feared, would stay with him for the rest of his life. His mind kept repeating the same stark question: why hadn't he told her before the wedding?

He knew instantly that the affair was over. Brought to a sudden, shuddering halt by his own stupidity. But he wasn't worried about the end of the affair. What he was distraught about were the other possible repercussions from his actions. He tried to think logically. What would be the point of her causing trouble later? No point at all. She had got her revenge at the church. He remembered the look on her face again and broke out into a cold sweat. *Did*, he wondered, *women think rationally*? Was this the end of the matter? He desperately hoped so. After all, he had never said anything about marriage. But the shell shock he felt would not go away. Mandy, at all costs, must never find out.

'Right, if you two lovebirds would like to get out, we're here,' said Jim jocularly from the driver's seat as they reached their destination.

Sue felt betrayed and humiliated as she drove back to her flat. She had partly got her own back but it wasn't enough – not nearly enough. Her fertile mind still reverberated from the massive shock to her pride. The painful realisation that she had not only lost control of the situation but had, in fact, never been in control was a new experience for her and a bitter pill to swallow. The tears streamed down her face as soon as she closed her front door. She rushed for some more paper handkerchiefs to try to stem the flow but the tears still kept on coming. She lay down on the bed – the bed where they had made love so often – her misery complete as she cried herself to sleep.

She woke feeling tired, irritable and hungry. She looked at her watch – it showed six thirty. Two hours' sleep was all she had managed. She hauled herself up and went into the kitchen and cooked herself a meal of pasta and minced beef. It was the first solid food she had consumed in over twenty-four hours. It satisfied her hunger but the deep pain inside her still blanketed all her thoughts. Sue already knew what she was going to do once they got back from their honeymoon. She opened a can of strong lager – the one that Peter liked best – and poured it into a pint beer mug. It was a long time since she had got really drunk and this seemed an opportune moment to repeat the experience. A romantic cassette, not played for a long time, caught her eye. She switched the light off and closed her eyes. The slow ballad soothed her jangling nerves. Sue was convinced about one thing. Peter John Carpenter was by the time she had finished with him going to wish he had never set eyes on her.

Peter didn't want to spoil the party but he did have a most dreadful headache and he badly needed a lie-down. He had made a speech, which wasn't a complete disaster, but everything was such an ordeal.

'Peter, they've got a room for you to rest in if you're feeling rough,' said Kay.

'Thanks, I think I will lie down for a few minutes – my head is bursting.'

'I've got some pills for you as well; you'd better take two.'

He suddenly felt an overwhelming urge to tell Kay the whole sordid truth but he rejected the idea almost as soon as he had thought of it.

She passed him the pills with a glass of water. 'At least you're not driving to Heathrow tonight.'

'I'll be fine tomorrow, Kay. Just let me lie here for a few minutes, it's only a headache.'

Peter drove them back to the house. Mandy was making coffee when Peter realised that he had forgotten to carry her over the threshold. Too late now, he reflected, but a pity all the same.

'At what time do we need to leave tomorrow?' asked Mandy as she brought the steaming hot coffee into the living room.

'About eight thirty, I think. We need to get there in plenty of time.'

'I hope you're feeling better,' said Mandy, looking concerned.

'A little, but I'm going to bed in a minute. I've still got a splitting headache. Sorry to be such a damp squib on our wedding night.'

'I've got something to tell you, Peter.'

'What's that?'

'I've stopped taking the pill,' announced Mandy, smiling broadly.

He felt his gloom and despondency lift temporarily as he smiled back at her. He reached out and took hold of her thin, elegant, long-fingered hand, drew it to his lips and kissed it.

'Your hands were made for playing the piano, have you ever tried?'

'No, I haven't, but I could always learn.'

He longed to ease his troubled mind by confessing everything but he knew he was not brave enough to take the risk. What a mad fool he had been to risk everything for a sexual fling. He felt himself over-come with remorse and guilt.

They had a trouble-free flight and the taxi journey to the hotel was hair-raising and eventful but happily accident-free. The large hotel was adequate and very soon they were ready and eager to go exploring. The largest city in the world was, as usual, heaving. Millions of cars taxis and lorries crammed the streets emitting toxics fumes. The excel-lent underground Metro was the salvation from total gridlock above ground.

'Apparently you can only drive your car on certain days of the week,' said Peter.

'Well, there still seem to be plenty about,' said Mandy, laughing.

'They clearly don't worry about anything as elementary as an annu-al MOT test,' said Peter as another lorry passed by in a cloud of black smoke.

They only had three days in Mexico City before they were to set off for the coast. So they were determined to make the most of them.

The smog obliterated some of the view but they could see most of the massive city home to over twenty million people from the fifty-second floor of La Latino. Mandy hugged Peter as they gazed over the giant metropolis, built 7,000 feet above sea level – urban density visi-ble as far as the eye could see. They looked towards the south-east and saw the towering, snow-covered still active Popocatepétl volcano standing majestically at 18,000 feet high.

'What a wonderful view, I must take some photos,' exclaimed Mandy.

Their visit to Guadalupe, the heart and soul of Catholic Mexico, they found to be a humbling experience. The Old Basilica and the New Basilica stood side by side with a large square in front. This holy place is a Mecca for tens of millions of pilgrims from all corners of

Mexico who visit throughout the year. Inside the New Basilica there was room for ten thousand worshippers, with Mass being taken all through the day and night. On their final night they sat entranced as they witnessed the incredible skills of the world famous dancers at the Bellas Artes. Now they were more than ready for the heat and sun of Acapulco.

There were so many coach firms to choose from that Peter and Mandy found it difficult to make a decision.

'It's a six-hour journey so let's travel in style. They all seem reasonable anyway,' said Peter as he worked out how many pesos there were to the dollar.

'The peso is very weak against the dollar, I'm glad we didn't bring pounds,' said Peter.

They didn't spend much time watching the on-board films but the bar facilities and the coffee were more enticing. The scenery was breathtaking especially when they neared Acapulco.

'That was very enjoyable,' said Mandy as they waited for a taxi.

The heat was scorching but, to their relief, it was a dry heat. After a short journey in a taxi their enormous hotel came into view. They were soon in their room, standing on their balcony and admiring the tranquil blue sea in front of them and golden, sandy beaches stretching as far as the eye could see.

They were anxious to be on the beach as soon as possible. Peter put on his brief swimming trunks and Mandy experimented with her new, daring, dark blue bikini.

'Are you going topless?' asked Peter, grinning at her.

'No, I'm not, Peter, I don't think that's quite me.'

The beach was almost deserted as Mandy rushed into the clear sea.

'The water is so warm and clean, Peter, come on in,' shouted Mandy as Peter was still stranded on the beach getting the sun loungers into position. He soon joined her and they swam joyfully in the calm sea. After that it was time to relax on the loungers.

'This sun is so powerful,' said Peter as they lay, roasting, a few yards from the water's edge liberally applying the strongest suntan lotion.

'You see that shady tree over there, Peter. We'll lie under that a little later. One hour in this sun will be more than enough.'

'I can't understand why there aren't more people about,' said Peter as he looked at acres and acres of nearly deserted sandy beach.

'Perhaps this isn't the peak season,' suggested Mandy. 'Anyway it looks as though these beaches go on for miles. This is paradise, Peter.'

Safely ensconced under a palm tree that offered some protection from the strong sun, sipping a ice-cold Coke purchased from an itinerant Mexican beach trader, Peter had only partly recovered from the dramatic confrontation at the wedding. The lingering doubts and apprehension still played relentlessly on his mind. Mandy was deliriously happy and they had made love every night since they had left England. She wanted a baby as much as he did. Why, he wondered, was he torturing himself with worries that would probably never materialise? They were in an amazing tropical resort with their whole lives in front of them. This, he knew only too well, should be one of the happiest times of his life. Sadly, he was besieged by fears that the beautiful woman he had tricked and lied to was planning her revenge. The look on her face still haunted him. He would have to see her as soon as he got back and he was not looking forward to the encounter!

'Let's go for a walk along the sands,' said Mandy as she grew restless sunbathing in the strong afternoon sun.

'It gets much hotter in summer,' a young Mexican girl cheerfully told them as they walked hand in hand along the shoreline, dipping their toes into the tepid water.

'Really! That's much too hot for me. It's probably all right for you Mexicans as you're used to this heat.'

'No, señor, it is too hot for me as well. I do not come here in the summer,' she replied smiling.

Peter estimated she was about eighteen. He took off his newly acquired sombrero and fanned himself.

'I think it's time to go back and sit under the palm trees again, Mandy. I could do with an ice cream as well. Keep an eye out for anybody selling them.'

Buying things on the beach was easy as there was no shortage of resourceful, poor Mexicans prepared to sell anything from chewing gum to coconuts.

They ate out at a different restaurant every night. Mostly light, spicy food with the humble tortilla a novelty for them both. The ice cream and various sorts of bread were their favourites but it was too hot to eat large meals.

The week passed too quickly. The heat was relentless but the resort exhilarating. At night the temperature refused to fall below seventy degrees Fahrenheit. The air conditioning was imperative otherwise sleeping would have been almost impossible. In the day the sun shone from a cloudless sky with the temperature soaring to over ninety degrees in the shade.

'It was a fab idea of yours to come here, darling. It's been fantastic.'

'It was nothing, Mandy – any genius could have done it,' replied Peter modestly.

'The only pity is we've got to leave,' said Mandy as they looked out from their balcony for the last time. Mandy turned away, took off her bikini and looked approvingly at her dark tan in the mirror. 'They'll be mighty envious of me at work when we get back,' she added laughing.

Back in the capital they had two days to kill before flying home. Time to buy some presents and sample the busy street life and experience how cheap everything was compared to their own country. Fortuitously they had avoided the dreaded Montezuma's revenge but now they took a chance as they sampled some delicious food from the multitude of street vendors: tacos, tostadas and more tortillas, the staple diet of poor Mexicans. The friendly people made them feel welcome and there was even time for Mandy to be serenaded by a wandering group of mariachis.

'I love the people but it's a shame there is such disparity between rich and poor,' said Mandy sadly.

She spotted a young woman, with a toddler playing in the grime by her feet, selling watches at bargain prices on a street corner. Peter saw Mandy's eyes get wider and larger as she tried on one she liked. She decided to buy it. She pulled out some notes from her handbag. The young woman clearly didn't speak any English.

'She can see you're a gringo,' said Peter.

'Quiet, Peter, everything is so incredibly cheap.'

'Watch out it hasn't fallen off the back of a lorry.'

Mandy ignored him and continued her negotiations. She held up four fingers and showed the young woman four ten peso notes. Mandy pointed to the watch she was holding and the woman's face broke into a smile. Mandy had secured a deal. She put it into her handbag and grinned at Peter.

'Not bad for a beginner, Peter.'

'I just hope it's still working tomorrow.'

'Oh, shut up! How much have I spent in English money?'

'About £6.'

A look of satisfaction appeared on her face.

'You wouldn't have been able to have completed that deal without your vast experience working in the bank – would you?'

'I think I did very well – it's a lovely watch.'

They waited patiently for the taxi to arrive. The airport was nearly half an hour drive's away but they had plenty of time. They had learnt that the Mexicans were not always punctual and had allowed extra time. The taxi arrived, a mere ten minutes late, and soon they were on their way.

'I'm going to give the sombrero to Jim,' said Peter, pleased to see Mandy smile in agreement. Beneath his geniality remained a deep foreboding about what lay ahead when they returned to Devon. Grave misgivings still dominated his thoughts. He feared the young woman that he had been infatuated with for several months. Now, after the adventure of a lifetime, it was time to go home and face the music.

Chapter Eight

Peter had endured a restless night. The flight back to England had been delayed by a couple of hours, which had led to a late arrival back home. Now he could only think of one thing. He urgently needed to see Sue as soon as possible. The best plan, he deduced, was to go round to her flat after she had returned from work. He was too terrified to phone and she might slam the phone down anyway. He hoped he could calm her down in a one-to-one situation. Wednesday was a good night to go round as she invariably stayed in. *Yes*, he thought, *tonight would be the best night to go.* Mandy stirred beside him and opened her eyes. She looked worn out and not at her best.

'You kept me awake last night. Every time I woke up you were awake and moving about,' said Mandy, rubbing the little sleep she had had from her eyes and yawning profusely. 'Thank goodness we don't have to go to work today. Are you worried about something, Peter?'

'No, of course not. Probably it's all the travelling – jet lag, I expect.'

Mandy roused herself and climbed out of bed, putting on her gold dressing gown. 'I'm going to have a shower and then get some breakfast. What do you want?'

Peter didn't feel hungry at all. 'I'll just have a cup of tea and a glass of orange juice please, Mandy.' He stayed limp in bed as he heard the water start up in the bathroom when she switched on the shower. He felt drained and listless – dreading the confrontation that loomed before him. But he knew he had no choice as the thought of Mandy finding out terrified him. He would have to be as diplomatic as possible; he must, at all costs, try to placate Sue. He remembered that look outside the church – how could he ever forget it? He closed his eyes, trying to erase it from his mind but try as he might the image would not go away. He wanted to go back to sleep but he knew that was going to be impossible. The meeting was probably only a few hours away. He searched his mind frantically for the key to save himself.

Peter saw her car parked almost outside her flat. At least, he reasoned, she was at home. Many times during the previous two and a half weeks he had planned what he was going to say to her. Now he felt almost paralysed with fear and apprehension. He parked his car a short distance away. His mouth felt dry as he approached her door and a feeling of trepidation and helplessness gripped him. He rang the bell, wondering if she was expecting him. It seemed to take an age for the door to open. Finally he heard the handle turn. She only opened it a fraction but it was sufficient for him to see the damage he had inflicted. He saw her dab her eyes with a handkerchief. They were blood red!

'I knew you'd come, Peter.'

'Sue, can I... can I come in and talk to you?'

She shook her head and put the handkerchief to her nose, blowing hard.

'Look, just let me come in for a moment. It's important. I need to talk to you. Please let me in, Sue.' He felt his voice rise as he sensed her intransigence.

'I never want to see you near my flat again.'

'Look, I was planning to tell you but the time never seemed right.' He saw a look of disdain cross her face.

'You had been going out with her for twelve months.'

'I wanted to tell you – honestly I did.'

'Sod off, Peter. Don't ever come here again.'

'Why won't you let me explain? We were never going to get married anyway.'

'What is there to talk about? Nothing! Go back to your wife, you swine. I hope I never see you again.'

He pushed hard at the door but the chain held firm. He pulled away and she took the opportunity to slam the door violently in his face.

Sue flung herself on the bed and cried her heart out. The wounds suffered so recently now ripped wide open again but her agony, this time, was short-lived. His increasing desperation only too obvious to her, it was now abundantly clear that her plan would not have to be modified. She would not try to implement it immediately but she would bide her time and wait until next week.

Sue could see that Peter's car was not in the driveway or parked in the road. This was the third time she had driven past the house. On the other two occasions she had seen Peter's car in the driveway. She presumed that the Mini, now parked in the driveway, was his wife's car. Apprehension gripped her but her resolve did not weaken. She was fearful he might return at any minute so there was no time to lose. She parked her car in a side road and walked purposefully back to the house. She rang the bell and she heard the sound of footsteps inside. What on earth would she do, she wondered, if Peter answered the door? The door opened and to her relief, Mandy, with an apron wrapped round her waist, greeted her.

'Hello, Sue, have you come with the photographs? Come in, I was washing the dishes. It's hard work being a married woman.'

The warm greeting unsettled Sue but her determination stayed firm.

'Yes, I've got the photos. They've come out very well.' She handed them over to Mandy who immediately took them out of the folder.

'Please, come in, Sue.' Mandy gestured for Sue to take a seat on the settee while she perused the photos.

'These are really lovely, Sue. Thanks for doing such a great job.'

'Will Peter be back soon, Amanda?'

'He's gone to see his mother in Totnes, I'm afraid. He won't be back for some time. I'm sorry you've missed him.'

Sue had not been in the house for many weeks but she noticed the whole room had been rearranged. Mandy looked a picture of health. Her rosy complexion, silky blonde hair and clear eyes radiating happiness. The impressive tan showed no sign of fading. Mandy put the photographs back in the folder.

'I'm sure Peter will be as thrilled with the photos as me,' said Mandy.

'Did you enjoy your honeymoon in Mexico? You've got a marvellous tan.'

'Yes, it was wonderful. We had a great time. The weather was fantastic and the people very friendly. I'd like to go back one day.'

Sue felt her pain return with a vengeance. She had no wish to hurt this girl but she felt unable to stop herself. 'I'm glad Peter is not here, Amanda. I need to have a private chat with you.' Sue noticed a puzzled expression appear on Mandy's face. 'There's something you need to know about Peter and me.'

'What do you mean?'

'Peter has been having an affair with me for the last six months. I didn't know about you until the day before the wedding when my boss asked me to take the wedding photographs.'

The colour had drained from Mandy's face instantly and she was as white as a sheet. Sue felt compelled to reach over and touch her lightly on the arm. Mandy started sobbing.

'It's not true – it can't be true. He wouldn't do that. Why are you saying these horrible things?' she pleaded between the sobs.

Sue got up and paced round the room looking down at her rival, distraught and tearful, still seated with her hands clutching her face.

'He's hurt me as well, Amanda. I thought you should know,' said Sue, feeling the need to justify her actions. She could see only too clearly the utter devastation she had caused as Mandy searched for answers.

'I don't understand. He loves me. Why would he have an affair with you?'

'That's something you'll have to ask him yourself. He lied to me. He humiliated me and I can't forgive him for that. You can have him as far as I am concerned. I never want to see him again.' Sue felt the anger start to subside as she gazed out of the large picture window on to the flower beds and neatly mown lawn. She had done the dirty deed. She didn't feel any joy at what she had done but she knew she had evened the score.

'I'm going now, Amanda. I can see myself out. I don't want to destroy your marriage, he's your husband, not mine.' She looked down at Mandy, a picture of confusion and shock, sitting on the large settee with her head in her hands – disconsolate and miserable. Mandy did not look up or say goodbye. Sue walked to the front door, opened it and stepped outside taking a deep breath of air. As far as she was concerned the matter was closed. It was time to look to the future. It was time to look for another man.

Peter parked his car in front of Mandy's. At last he was starting to relax as, thankfully, his worst fears had not been realised. He wondered what she would have cooked for his supper and decided he would put the car in the garage later. He opened the front door, wondering why all the lights were off. Surely Mandy had not gone to bed.

He slowly opened the living room door and looked inside. As soon as he saw her, curled up in a ball lying motionless on the settee, his heart sank. He knew only too well what had transpired. He walked slowly over to her and touched her damp cheeks tenderly and ran his fingers down the side of her smooth face until he reached her neck. She did not look at him and spoke quietly.

'She came to see me, Peter.'

'I feared she might, darling.'

'Why did you do it? You said you loved me. If that's true why did you need her? Please tell me.'

Peter felt a feeling of inadequacy and self-loathing spread within him. He wanted to heal the gaping wound.

'I do love you, Mandy, more than anything in the world. She wasn't important to me. You must forgive me – please say you do. I was going to end it anyway.'

'I still don't understand why you wanted her if you say you love me.'

He knew the truth would hurt her too much so he felt the need to prevaricate.

'She led me on and I didn't have the strength to end it. I wish I had ended it. I'd do anything to turn the clock back. It won't happen again – I promise you. You mean everything to me. I was a fool to get involved with her but I've learnt my lesson. You must trust me.'

Finally she looked at him and kissed him on the cheek. She nestled her head against his chest as he put his arm tightly around her. They did not speak. He felt a great sense of relief but his uneasiness remained. He knew he had deeply hurt her. Would he ever be able to repair the damage caused by his own recklessness and selfishness? He knew he loved her; that surely, he reasoned, was the most important thing.

Peter was feeling tense and worried. Christmas had been a low-key affair with Mandy seemingly unable to join fully in the festivities. She hadn't mentioned his affair since that terrible day, weeks before, when she had found out, but surely that was the catalyst that was making her morose and lethargic. He had tried everything to coax her out of her despondency but with no real success. He had persuaded her to go and see her doctor, who had prescribed her pills, but she was still far from the happy, smiling, contented young woman he had married less than three months before. He desperately needed to talk with Kay and Jim. Kay, in particular, might have the key to unlock the padlocked door. He phoned when Mandy was out at her parents' house. Kay had seemed as anxious to see him as he was to see her and invited him to come and see her.

Kay was dressed in thick dark brown trousers and a warm polo-necked sweater to guard against the late-December winter cold. She opened the front door and greeted him with a smile. He removed his scarf and dark overcoat and hung them on the rail just inside the front door. Jim was warming his hands on one of the gas radiators as Kay led the way into the lounge.

'It's bloody freezing today,' said Jim, trying to breathe some life back into his frozen fingers.

'Have you been working outside today?' asked Peter.

'You bet we have. We self-employed builders can't afford to take two and a half weeks off for Christmas, you know.'

'Where are you working at the moment?'

'We're finishing off this house in Chelston. It was dry today but I think I may have got frostbite. We carried on until dark. I need to finish that house to get paid.'

'Your lasagne is in the microwave,' announced Kay.

'Good, I'm absolutely starving, I could eat a horse.'

'Do you want anything, Peter?' asked Kay.

'Just a cuppa, Kay, please.'

She disappeared to the kitchen but soon returned with a mug of hot tea. 'I've put two sugars in,' she said as she handed him a teaspoon. 'Do you want one of these Terry's All Gold chocolates?'

'No thanks, Kay, not just at the moment.' Peter wanted to get straight to the point. He saw Kay sitting opposite him, looking pensive. 'Mandy is a bit down at the moment,' he said.

'I think that's the understatement of the year, Peter. The poor girl is very unhappy.'

'I sent her to the doctor to see if she could help her.'

'How very thoughtful of you – trying to clear up a mess of your own making.'

'I've told her I'm sorry.'

'What a stupid thing to do, Peter, but I expect you realise that now.' She stopped momentarily as if gathering her thoughts. Peter saw her take a deep breath. 'She's a very sensitive girl. She was very hurt when she found out. Come to think of it, how do you think I feel as I was the one who brought you together? You let me down as well, you know.'

'Yes, I know. I've messed the whole thing up.'

'Look, Peter, I know how fond you are of Mandy, I've told her that, but you'll have to be patient and wait for her to get over it.'

'It's been over two months. How long is it going to take?'

'How long is a piece of string, Peter? Be patient. I'll do my best to help. I don't want the two of you to break up.'

Peter felt panic-stricken! 'What has she been saying about breaking up?' he asked urgently.

He saw Kay bite her lip.

'She's very fragile at the moment. Give her time and I'm sure everything will be fine.'

Peter felt the tension inside him ease slightly as he picked up his mug of tea. It was now only lukewarm but it eased the dryness in his throat. He still wanted to know more.

'Has she talked to you about how hurt she is?'

'Not exactly, but I can feel it. You let her down. Why did you do it?'

He had been waiting for this but it still irritated him when it finally came. He couldn't bring himself to tell her the truth.

'I wish I knew. I'd give anything to turn the clock back but unfortunately it can't be done. Don't tell her I've talked to you, will you?'

'No, I won't. We never had this conversation.'

They were interrupted by the sound of Jim shouting from the dining room that he had finished the lasagne. He opened the lounge door to emphasise the point.

'Do you want some gateau?' Kay offered.

'Yes please, a big piece, and a cup of coffee.'

Kay picked up Peter's mug and smiled. Peter felt envious. His best friend's marriage was in a much healthier state than his own.

Mandy was getting agitated. Peter wanted to go out for a meal but she was digging her heels in and maintaining she didn't want to go. They had reached stalemate but Peter was not prepared to give up.

'Why don't you want to go out tonight?' he asked for the third time, finding himself becoming exasperated.

'Because I don't feel like it. I'd rather stay in.'

'You never seem to want to go anywhere with me these days,' he added, knowing he was only throwing petrol onto the smouldering fire.

'I'm not going out with you tonight and that's final,' she replied firmly, her face becoming flushed.

'I suppose we'll have to stay in and watch the rubbish on the telly again. That *EastEnders* drives me up the wall.'

'Go down the pub on your own, I'm not bothered.'

'Okay, that's suits me fine.' He picked up his car keys from the living room table and stuffed them in his pocket.

'Don't take the car if you're going to drink, Peter. You should know better than that.'

He reached into his pocket and pulled the keys out again and threw them on the floor.

'Right, I'll bloody well walk. I don't know what time I'll be back.'

'You can stay out all night, as far as I'm concerned, if you're going to behave like a spoilt child,' said Mandy.

Peter slammed the front door behind him. The light drizzle and cold wind bit into his face but he didn't notice. He anticipated coming home the worse for wear. Probably he would sleep on the sofa; this time he was sure she would leave him there all night.

A few days later Peter had the bright idea of trading in his four-year-old Escort for an almost new pale green Escort. He drove it home feeling pleased with himself and felt sure Mandy would be as excited with his purchase as he was. It soon became clear that she most certainly wasn't.

'The company gives me an allowance for the car so it's not costing too much,' insisted Peter.

'We're not as well off as you seem to think, Peter. We still have to pay off a substantial mortgage and what happens if the rate goes up? My money is supposed to be for a larger house if we need one.'

'I've thought of all that—'

She interrupted him sharply. 'If we have a baby I might want to give up work. The old car was perfectly all right.'

'I should be able to spend some of my money if I want to.' He closed his eyes as he waited for her response.

'You should have discussed it with me first. We are married now, you know.'

'I wanted it to be a surprise. I got a very good part exchange deal on the old Escort.'

'I don't care about that, Peter.'

'I can't do anything right as far as you're concerned. Don't you trust me?'

He saw her facial expression change as she pulled out a paper handkerchief from her trouser pocket and wiped her eyes. They were moist but blazing.

'How dare you say that after what you did to me!'

Peter could see all the pain return as she released all the bottled-up emotions that had been trapped inside her. She blew loudly into her handkerchief as she tried to regain her control. He instinctively rushed towards her and put his arm round her shoulder.

'Look, I'm sorry about the car. It was thoughtless and stupid of me. Please forgive me.'

She wiped her eyes with her hand, looked into his eyes and put her arms round his neck, kissing him on the lips. She was smiling – the old passion briefly rekindled. He squeezed her hard as he had done so many times before. He hoped this was the turning point in their disintegrating relationship. How he wanted the old Mandy back. He knew he wanted that more than anything he had ever wanted in his life before. Kay had told him to be patient but he was finding it so hard. He knew this was a critical moment in their life together and vowed to wait as long as it took. He knew she was the only woman he had ever loved.

That night they made love for the first time in many days. He wanted to make her pregnant; that would, he was sure, cement their marriage and give Mandy a new focus to direct her love and vitality. They had both wanted a baby right from the start, but her periods had continued as normal. More patience, he repeated to himself; it was just a question of more patience.

But it was a false dawn and soon her depression returned stronger than ever. As the February days lengthened so her moods darkened. She refused to go to work and moped around the house for days on end pleading persistent migraines or an upset stomach. The dreadful weather made things worse with the wind and the rain unrelenting. Torrential rain and gales blew in from the south-west as winter tightened its ugly grip. Mandy had just returned from a long appointment with her doctor when she dropped the bombshell.

'Peter, I need to be away from you for a bit. I want to go back to live with Mum and Dad.'

Peter was not totally surprised, he had been half-expecting it for weeks. He felt mortified but resigned. She threw her sopping wet black raincoat on to an armchair and sat down beside him on the settee.

'My mind's made up and I'm not going to change it.'

'But you said you loved me a few weeks ago.'

'I'm confused, Peter. I'm not sure any more. My head is going round in circles and driving me insane. I can't think or work properly. Perhaps we can get together again later but I need to be alone now.'

All the fight had drained out of him. He could see it was pointless to argue. He remembered the last time they had made love – only ten days before. Another false dawn he reflected bitterly. His life, recently, was full of false dawns.

'Do you want me to come and see you?' he asked, clutching at straws.

'No, I don't. I need a complete break. I don't feel well at all. The doctor has increased my prescription and signed me off work for a month. I promise I'll contact you as soon as I'm ready.'

'When are you going?'

'As soon as Dad can get a van to take my stuff away.'

Peter nodded but said nothing as he could see the whole operation had been meticulously planned. He felt desolate but he could see she was adamant.

'Your mum will be pleased – she always hated me.'

'That's not true, Peter. Please don't bring my mother into this.'

'I'll sleep in the spare room tonight, Mandy. Can you make the bed up for me?' He walked out into the hall. Tomorrow, perhaps, she would be gone and he would be alone. Alone, he pondered, to speculate on his own contribution to his predicament. The lovely young woman whom he worshipped and adored was walking out on him. He picked up a pencil lying on the desk, snapped it in half with all the force he could muster, and threw the pieces in the waste bin. An empty gesture, he knew, but a sign of his growing frustration at the knowledge that the situation he found himself in was entirely of his own making.

He left for work the following morning with a heavy heart. Mandy was still asleep and he had not bothered to wake her. The whole day was dominated by one thought in his mind. Would she still be there when he returned from work? He stopped at a pub on the way home. Half of him wanted to go home and see if she was still there. The other half was terrified to go home in case she wasn't.

He sat alone at the bar. A half of lager turned into another half and then another. Even the barman gave up on him as Peter's thoughts were miles away. Perhaps she had had a change of heart overnight. Perhaps her father had not managed to get hold of a van. His thoughts went back to when he had asked her to marry him. It seemed only yesterday, and they were so much in love. He steeled himself for what possibly awaited him at home. He left without a word to the barman and took his car keys out of his jacket pocket.

When he turned into his driveway his heart sank. Her car was nowhere to be seen and the drive was deserted. He opened the front door and saw her house keys lying on the doormat. He picked them up, kissed them, and put them in his trouser pocket. He could feel the tears streaming down his face but could not find the strength to wipe them away. Frantically he rushed upstairs and opened the wardrobes to find that everything of hers was gone. He searched the whole house for a note. He did not find one.

Chapter Nine

The telephone rang just as Sue was standing precariously on the steps brushing emulsion onto her kitchen ceiling. She cursed the timing of the interruption but curiosity got the better of her and she hastily grabbed hold of an old discarded tunic to wipe her hands. Her worst fears were realised when it was Barry. Why, she wondered, had she been so stupid as to give him her telephone number?

'Hello, Sue, how are you?'

'Fine – but I'm busy painting the kitchen ceiling at the moment.'

'Okay, I'll only keep you a second. Did you enjoy last Monday?'

'Oh yes, Barry, it was lovely,' she lied convincingly.

'Do you want to come out again next Tuesday? I know a good pub with Country and Western music.'

'I don't think so. I'm going out with someone else at the moment.' She didn't want to hurt his feelings and thought it best to tell a white lie.

He sounded disappointed. 'Oh right, I didn't realise. Perhaps I'll give you a ring again some time then.'

'Yes, do that. I'll see you some time.'

Sue filled up the electric kettle and waited for it to boil. A cup of tea was what she unquestionably needed and the painting was put on hold for a few minutes. She winced as she recalled the unfortunate tedious goings-on in Barry's dingy unkempt bedsit on Monday night. One night in that hovel, his eager hands caressing her body was one night too many. If he had bothered to take a shower before starting his clumsy seduction, the experience might have been marginally more tolerable but overall, she reflected, she would have had more fun staying at home with a hot-water bottle. With a bit of luck she had put him off for good, but if he did ring again she would have to be more direct.

She looked at her watch. Philip would be round in just over two hours to show her some photographs he had taken a few days before.

Apparently he wanted her opinion on whether they were good enough to submit to an exhibition in London. She knew he had a taste for small cakes so she took the ones she had bought from the baker's earlier that morning out of the bag, ready to serve.

Now she turned her attention back to the painting. If she got her skates on there was just time for her to finish the ceiling, clean herself up, find some decent clothes and make herself presentable. She gulped down the tea, picked up her paintbrush and methodically continued with her task. She let out a tiny giggle. What on earth would Philip think of her, she wondered, if he could see what she looked like in her paint-covered clothes and old battered plastic hat? She was working faster now, with a one and a half hour's deadline to meet and a spring-clean of the kitchen uppermost in her mind. The warm March sunshine streamed in through the kitchen window as she worked, signalling that spring had well and truly arrived.

Sue pulled hard as she untangled her hair with a comb and then brushed it into shape. She looked in the mirror at the cream skirt and matching top she had just put on. *That*, she thought, *will do nicely*. She was searching for her lipstick when the doorbell rang.

'Drat the man,' she muttered under her breath as she saw he was a few minutes early.

'What a lovely smell of paint,' said Philip as she ushered him into the living room.

'I've just finished. Do you want to have a look?'

They moved to the kitchen so that they could both admire her handiwork.

'Very professional,' he remarked, grinning from ear to ear. She let out a giggle. 'Apart from that little bit on the corner.' He pointed at the offending mark on the ceiling about an inch wide. Her smile got wider.

'I left that deliberately to see if you'd notice.'

'I like the colour, Sue. The whole thing matches very nicely. You're a real artist.'

Sue wasn't quite sure if he was being sarcastic but she decided to give him the benefit of the doubt.

'Let's go into the living room and see what you've been doing, Philip.'

He quickly produced the photographs from his briefcase and she scoured them for imperfections, but couldn't find any.

'These photos are smashing. The lady in them looks about fifty.

Did you take them in her home?'

'Yes, in Dawlish. She's very photogenic. Do you think they're good enough?'

'Yeah, I think they are. When is the exhibition?'

'The week starting 13 May. I was thinking of going up to London for a few days. I can stay with my mother in Leytonstone.'

'Why not? You work very hard and hardly take any time off. We can cope perfectly well on our own. Do you want some tea?'

'Yes please, Sue, I haven't had time for any lunch.'

Sue excused herself and went to get the refreshments. She soon returned with tea and the cakes which Peter started on as if he hadn't eaten for a week and she watched in awe as the large plate of cakes steadily disappeared. She surveyed him intently, his receding hairline and growing waistline a sign of middle age as he approached his fortieth birthday.

'You're not going to make yourself ill eating all my cakes,' said Sue.

'I told you I didn't have any lunch.'

'Is it Laura's turn to have the boys this weekend?'

'Yeah, it is. They come to me next weekend.'

'How long is it since you got divorced?'

'Almost five years. Clive's twelve and Matt's ten. It's a pity they don't live in Torbay but Taunton is not too far away.'

'Neither of you have got married again?'

She saw his face tighten. 'Laura's going out with someone – he's an engineer working for Somerset County Council. It wasn't me that wanted the divorce and I found it a very painful experience. She was only twenty when we got married – much too young. I miss not seeing the boys more often.'

'We've known each other for nearly three years and it's the first time you've told me all this.' She could see he wanted to change the subject.

'What about you, Sue? I thought you were going to marry that guy from Torquay.'

'It was never that serious, Philip. I'm still on the right side of thirty. I'm sure I won't get left on the shelf.'

'I never for one moment thought you would be,' said Philip.

She poured him a third cup of tea as she saw another cake move to his plate.

'These cakes are exceedingly good – are they Mr Kiplings?' he asked.

She laughed. 'Whoever's they are they're nearly all gone. I was hoping to have one or two for my tea tomorrow but that plan has gone out of the window.'

'Sorry, I thought you put them out for me to eat.'

'Pass me one before you scoff the lot.'

He passed the plate to her, smiling. She wanted to explore further.

'Do you go out much in the evenings?'

'Not very much. I don't go into pubs very often these days. I've got Sky Sports at home so I watch quite a bit of that. On Tuesday night I think I might go to Plainmoor and watch Torquay.'

He looked at her for a moment as though he was weighing something up in his mind. He smiled at her an infectious smile.

'I was just thinking, Sue.'

'What were you thinking, Philip?'

'Would you like to come?'

She was wide awake enough to contain her immediate compulsion to laugh hysterically. She even managed, with commendable restraint, to avoid a giggle. On the face of it, she knew, it was difficult to imagine anything she would rather do less. Her brain moved like greased lightning and she played for time.

'But I hate football,' she protested amiably, allowing a broad smile to cross her face.

'I just wondered if you might like to come. Don't worry if you don't.'

She felt herself becoming bolder. 'I'll come on one condition.'

'What's that?'

'That you take me to a nightclub on the following Saturday night.' She felt her heart beating faster as he seemed to take for ever to answer; he looked so serious.

Finally he smiled at her. 'Okay, it's a deal. Mind you, I don't think I've been to one of those places since before I married Laura and I expect I'll need to bring some earplugs.'

She smiled at him; a feeling of quiet satisfaction and excitement started to build within her. She had not contemplated a development such as this. She looked at him again. He was not too ancient – barely ten years older than she was. Some people, she reflected, might think he was still quite good-looking. She was already looking forward to Saturday. As for the wretched football, she was prepared to endure that.

She looked at the large plate where she had stacked the cakes. It was empty! Philip patted his stomach and wiped the crumbs away from his mouth.

'I must go, Sue. Thanks for the cakes. The way I feel at the moment I may forego supper. Make sure you wrap up warm for Tuesday.'

Philip and Sue walked briskly along Warbro Road towards the ground. The floodlights were already on although the daylight was only starting to turn to dusk.

'Do you think it's going to rain?' asked Sue anxiously.

'No the moon is out, there's no need for you to worry.'

Sue didn't believe a word of it and pulled the hood of her anorak over her head ready to combat any eventuality.

'It's very cold, Philip. We could freeze to death!'

'I hadn't noticed. Don't worry, the adrenalin and excitement will soon warm you up.'

'Where are we sitting?' asked Sue.

Philip let out a loud laugh.

'This isn't the Premier League; we're standing.'

Sue felt a little disappointed. *Still*, she thought, *it will make it easier for me to jump up and down to keep my feet warm.*

The whole of the first half passed so slowly. The unrelenting boredom scrambled her mind as she watched twenty-two grown men spit on the ground and shout at each other in a frenzy of endeavour. So much effort, she decided, but totally pointless. The referee placed the whistle in his mouth and a loud blast ensued. Everybody walked off the pitch and Sue turned on her heels, expecting Philip to follow. He called after her.

'Where are you going?'

She suddenly became aware that she had made a terrible mistake. 'Oh, sorry I forgot – there's more.'

Philip opened up a small bag he had been carrying over his shoulder and produced a flask. 'I don't usually bring anything but I thought you might be cold.'

Sue was grateful for any small mercies and the piercing March wind made her grateful she had cocooned herself in thick winter clothing.

'That's great, Philip, I could do with a hot drink.'

He carefully poured some tea into a plastic cup and handed it to her.

'How long do they have for their interval?' she asked.

'Fifteen minutes.'

'That long!'

'They need to discuss tactics. Torquay will be playing with the wind at their backs in the second half so we should see some goals. Their back four look a bit vulnerable to me. We need to get more people out wide and get behind them. Surely you can see that?'

She gave him a sharp kick on his shin. He reeled away clutching his ankle spilling his tea down the front of his trousers.

'Ow, that hurt! Now I've got a sore ankle and wet trousers.'

Sue thought of intervening with the help of a tissue but was worried the whole episode might be misconstrued. Philip recovered and poured himself some more tea.

'Serves you right for provoking me,' said Sue.

'Are you enjoying it?' asked Philip.

She decided to be diplomatic and sidestep the silly question. 'There doesn't seem to be many people here.'

'There's probably about two thousand. The ground's nearly full when we play Exeter or Plymouth.'

The players returned for the second half. Sue reached into her pocket and fished out a packet of mints. She offered one to Philip and then put her sheepskin gloves back on. Her poor feet, despite much stamping, felt like blocks of ice.

Ten minutes from the end the deadlock was broken. Torquay attacked and closed in on goal, a Torquay player fired in a shot that was probably destined to hit the corner flag, the ball struck another Torquay player on the knee and deflected wickedly past the helpless goalkeeper.

'Goal!' shouted a thousand people. There were scenes of joy and wild excitement as the players and spectators celebrated.

'Great goal,' said Peter, clapping his hands.

Even Sue with her extremely limited knowledge of the game could see it was a fluke but thought it wise not to say so. She rejoiced along with everybody else. Soon some people close by started whistling. Sue didn't like the noise.

'Why are people whistling, Philip?'

'They're telling the referee that it's time to end the match.'

'I can't understand that, surely the referee has got his own watch.'

'We badly need the three points. If we finish at the bottom of the division we drop into the Conference.'

'What's wrong with that? Surely it's sensible to have a conference if you're near the bottom of the division.'

Now Philip was whistling as well – perhaps it was contagious. Soon her fortitude was rewarded as the match ended. Everyone seemed very happy but Sue thought it extremely unlikely she would want to repeat the experience, even if the weather was warm and sunny.

The heating in Philip's dark red Rover soon allowed Sue to thaw out. He drove her straight home and they talked for ages in Sue's living room. She didn't try to seduce him. Somehow it didn't seem appropriate as they had been friends for so long. He did give her a brief kiss on the lips as he said goodnight to her but that was all. However, Sue knew she had a gorgeous new dress already hanging in her wardrobe. She wanted to look as stunning as possible on Saturday night.

The loud music blared out incessantly and the atmosphere was electric. The thudding monotonous beat was not conducive to speech but certain to make the heart beat faster and the feet tapping.

'I didn't expect to see an old man like you in a place like this,' said one of Philip's football chums as they both gyrated to the music.

'Who are you calling an old man, Ken? I can keep this up for hours,' said Philip, mopping his brow with his handkerchief.

Sue was glad that Philip had left his car outside her flat. Now they could enjoy themselves without the threat and inhibiting influence of the breathalyser. She was pleased to see Philip keep up a good pace despite being slightly unfit. It wasn't until eleven thirty that he started to show unmistakable signs of flagging.

'I think I'll just sit here and watch, Sue. I used to go for an early morning run when I was younger. Perhaps I'll have to start again.'

They walked out of the club, near the harbour in Torquay, almost on the stroke of midnight. The church clock sounded the start of a new day.

'Is this when I turn back into my usual boring self?' said Philip.

The air was cold and still as they looked for a taxi. A wailing police car roared past and stopped quickly a hundred yards further on.

'Another fight, I expect,' said Sue as they clambered into the back of a waiting taxi.

'That was exciting, but I'm not sure I'd want to do that too often. I've still got a ringing noise in my ears.'

Sue looked at Philip slumped beside her, seemingly worn out. 'You stayed longer than I thought you would.'

'Well, I feel shattered and I may need a week to recover. And I've had too much to drink so I won't be able to drive home. You're leading me into bad habits.'

Sue gave him a brief kiss on the cheek. The last thing she wanted was for him to drive home. The scruples of only a few nights before were now conveniently forgotten.

Sue woke early. She looked at Philip and saw he was fast asleep. The strenuous evening followed by energetic sex, Sue observed, had taken their toll. He didn't move a muscle as she slid quietly out of bed to visit the bathroom and get a drink of water. Soon she returned, slipping in deftly beside him anxious not to disturb him from his slumbers.

He had been a kind and considerate lover but she knew she still missed the naked passion she had enjoyed with the man she had spurned and now despised. It still hurt her to think about him so her thoughts returned to her most recent lover. She allowed herself a mischievous smile. Perhaps, with a little more tuition, she could teach Philip a few things about lovemaking. She would have to be careful; she didn't want to shock him too much. Sue drifted off to sleep again.

When she woke again she found she was suffering from hunger pains. *Not surprising*, she thought, when she looked at her watch and saw it was ten fifteen. She looked again at Philip and saw that he was still dead to the world. It was time for some breakfast.

Sue was busy in the kitchen when Philip finally surfaced. He walked in, yawning and stroking his face.

'So you've finally got your strength back, you poor old thing,' jeered Sue. 'You'll have to do better than this if you want to keep up with me.'

'I need a shave, Sue. I'm not used to waking up in a strange woman's bed but I must admit it does have some attractions.'

'I haven't got a razor but I can provide breakfast.'

'Can't I borrow your razor?'

'You must be kidding, Philip.'

'What cereal have you got?'

'I've got Weetabix or cornflakes.'

'I really wanted Sugar Puffs but the Weetabix will do. I'll have two, please, with some hot milk. You have got milk, haven't you? I can't see any in this fridge. Oh yes, I can see it now. Do you want some?'

'Okay, I'll have the same as you. There's a pan on top of the cooker. I'll go and get dressed.'

Sue pulled her navy blue sweater over her head, combed her hair and went back into the kitchen to join Philip. The cereal and spoons were already on the table. He poured her a fresh cup of tea.

'I get plenty of practice with this sort of thing when the boys come.'

'You've done very well but I think I need some toast. Do you want some?' She saw him nod.

'The boys will be coming down next weekend, Sue. Do you want to come over and get to know them better.'

She hesitated. This was the thing that bothered her the most. Of course she had seen them in the shop from time to time, but she was nervous about getting too involved with them. It was best to see how the relationship developed.

'I'm sorry, Philip, I'm going to be busy next weekend. I'd love to come another time.' She studied his face carefully to make sure he wasn't too disappointed. Luckily he didn't seem to be. 'How are they doing at school?'

'Pretty good. At least they don't have to put up with the wretched eleven-plus as we do in Torbay. They both learn quickly so perhaps they'll both end up at university.'

'I hope so. I daren't tell you what I got up to at Exeter University!' she replied.

'I can imagine it, Sue, I can imagine it. I sometimes wish I'd gone to university but you had to be really clever in my day. Besides I was keen to earn some money as my parents weren't well off. My brother passed the eleven-plus but I failed. Still I haven't done too badly.'

'You've built up a very successful business and done very well.'

He smiled and helped her clear the table and wash up.

'I'll see you at work tomorrow,' he said as he got ready to leave. He gave her a light kiss on the lips and picked up his jacket. His face broke into a wide grin.

'Don't worry, I won't ask you to come to any more football matches – you've suffered enough. You looked like a fish out of water.'

'That's a relief, Philip. I was just so cold and bored. But we can go to a club occasionally, can't we?'

He gave her a wink and another peck on the cheek.

'Yeah, I certainly wouldn't rule that out but I may have to get in some training first.'

The relationship did develop. So much so that Sue was thrilled, but not surprised, when Philip invited her to go to London with him for the May trip.

'Jenny can cope in the shop for a week and I can get Martin to help out on the Saturday when we're busy. I want you to come and meet my mother and brother.'

Sue was relieved she had her credit card debt under reasonable control but a week in London with Philip – the West End shops at her mercy – was likely to undermine the situation radically.

'I've brought an extra suitcase with me, I might need it,' she announced as Philip parked at Newton Abbot station.

'I'll get a car park disc in the booking office for when we come back, we've got plenty of time,' said Philip.

Sue waited on the platform, feeling pleased with herself. By booking well in advance they had cheap tickets and the bonus of reserved seats. The warm spring sunshine only served to increase her anticipation of the delights ahead, as the Plymouth to Paddington express arrived punctually.

'I'm sure Jenny will be able to deal with everything but I'd better phone and make certain,' said Philip as they made themselves comfortable. He reached into his jacket, pulled out his mobile phone and dialled.

'It's engaged, I'll try again in a few minutes.'

The train meandered slowly along the banks of the River Teign for a few miles until it reached the small holiday town of Teignmouth and then the sands and the open sea. Now the train gathered speed as the railway line ran parallel to the sea, only feet away, then on through the delightful, even smaller town, of Dawlish towards the city of Exeter. Now all eyes turned to see the panoramic views across the open sea to the much larger town of Exmouth. Soon, the open sea was left behind and the River Exe came into view followed quickly by the first stop, Exeter St David's.

'Well, that's the pretty part completed, let's see if I can get Jenny.'

This time he was more successful.

'The shop is as dead as the dodo this morning. She says she's bored. I hope it picks up this afternoon. Do you want some tea or coffee?'

'That would be nice. I'll have some coffee, please.'

Philip set off for the snack bar. He soon returned with coffee and biscuits.

'Did I tell you I've started going to this fitness club once a week?' said Philip.

'You know perfectly well you haven't told me. How long do you think you'll keep that up?'

'That's difficult to say but I've done two weeks so far.' He looked at his watch. 'The whole journey should take less than three hours. If it's on time we'll be there at about one. Time for a bite of lunch and then take a taxi to my mother's house. I told her not to get us any lunch today.'

'When did your father die?'

'Gosh, it must be seven years ago now. It was the year after they moved to Leytonstone to live with my grandfather. Dad died after a heart attack and then Grandfather died of lung cancer five and a half years ago. Since then Mum has lived on her own but luckily Tim, Jackie and Jessica live very close. I want you to meet my brother and his family.'

'How old is your brother?'

'Thirty-five, the same age as Jackie. Jessica is nine.'

They arrived at Paddington almost on time, had a quick snack in the station and then joined a long queue waiting for a taxi. The journey, through the heavy traffic to Leytonstone, took longer than expected and it was two thirty before they arrived at Philip's mother's house.

Sue estimated she was about sixty-five. A small woman with short, grey hair and a warm friendly smile. Her round face and thin glasses did not match. She seemed rather inquisitive.

'You must call me Janet, Sue,' she insisted as she introduced herself.

'You've known Philip several years I believe, dear,' she said as they sat down in the large, well-decorated lounge.

'Yes, just over three years. We work well together.'

'I always hoped he'd meet a nice girl again. The divorce was very unfortunate.'

Sue glanced up just in time to see Philip making a rude gesture from behind his mother's back.

'That dress is very nice, my dear, I suppose it's the fashion to wear them so short these days.'

'Well, Mrs… I mean Janet, the truth is I've got very good legs and I like showing them off.'

She looked up again and saw Philip holding both hands to his head and making a funny face at her. Meanwhile, his mother, she noted, had been rendered temporarily speechless.

'Mum, we're both dying for a cup of tea.'

'Oh, are you, darling? All right, I'll just pop out and make one.'

Janet, slightly red-faced, made her way out to the kitchen. Sue was glad of this as she wanted to clarify one or two things with Philip.

'Don't worry, Sue, you two will be fine together. She likes to know everything, that's all.'

They heard the sound of breaking china as something shattered on the kitchen floor, immediately followed by the utterance of an expletive. Sue rushed to help. Janet was on her hands and knees trying to pick up the pieces.

'Don't worry, my dear, I can clear the mess up. Can you pass me the dustpan and brush in that cupboard?'

Sue was relieved when peace and quiet were soon restored.

The exhibition was taking place near Victoria Station. This time they travelled by tube. Leytonstone Station to Liverpool Street on the Central line and then on to Victoria via the southbound Circle Line. After a five-minute walk they were there.

The standard of work was frighteningly high and Philip didn't win any prizes, but they weren't too disappointed. They spent an enjoyable couple of hours looking at the exhibits. Afterwards they had a quiet drink in a pub on Vauxhall Bridge Road before making the return journey. Tim, Jackie and Jessica were coming as soon as Jessica finished school. They didn't want to be late.

Tim was boyish-looking with longish dark brown hair. He had a thin face and Sue thought him average looking. Jackie was much shorter, a redhead with medium-length hair and a pleasant face. Jessica was plain with a gawky look and short dark brown hair. Sue thought that she might blossom as she grew older but she was not a pretty child.

'You didn't drive up, Phil?' asked Tim.

'No, you know how I hate driving in London. It was just as cheap for the two of us to come by train and a lot less hassle. We can get about better by tube and taxi.'

'Have you decided what you're doing tomorrow?' asked Jackie.

Sue jumped in. 'Tomorrow we're going shopping in the West End and then we're going to the theatre. We haven't decided which show but I've got one in mind. We want to have some fun, don't we, Philip?' She stopped suddenly. Why was everybody staring at her? Why was Jessica's mouth wide open?

'I'm getting a bit old for too much fun but I know what you mean,' said Philip.

'Jess, will you come and help me lay the table?' shouted Janet from the kitchen. Jessica made a face and reluctantly sauntered towards the dining room.

'This house is much too large for you, Mum,' said Tim as they all tucked into steak pie, mashed potatoes, carrots and broccoli. All, that is, except Jessica who proudly announced she was a vegan and was served a nut cutlet and the vegetables.

'I expect she'll soon grow out of it,' said her father.

Jessica saw her shoot a venomous look in his direction. She seemed a very determined young lady.

Sue was a little bit frustrated that Philip was finding it so difficult to keep up with her as they rushed headlong into one shop after another along Oxford Street. She saw him sit down on a chair for a brief respite.

'I think I may need to go to the gym twice a week rather than once,' said Philip. 'This pace is killing me.'

Sue chastised him. 'I only come to London once in a blue moon so I need to stock up. The theatre can look after these bags while we're watching the show. I've neatly finished now. Then we can look for a restaurant.'

They found one without too much bother.

'I've always wanted to see *Les Misérables*, it's in its sixteenth year, you know,' announced Sue as they started on the soup course.

'I would have preferred Elaine Page in *The King and I* but I'm happy with your choice,' said Philip wearily.

They arrived well in time at the Palace Theatre.

'These are really good seats, Philip,' said Sue as they waited for the curtain to go up.

Philip dozed off twice during the performance and when she shook him he protested that he was exhausted from all the shopping. He did manage to buy her a drink during the interval which she appreciated as it had been a strenuous day.

The next day was less frenetic. They got up late and didn't bother with breakfast.

Even Sue, her adrenalin spent, felt the after-effects of her obsession. A leisurely stroll round the Houses of Parliament and the view inside Westminster Abbey were relaxing. It was the first time either of them had been inside the Abbey.

'It dates back to the eleventh century when it was a Benedictine monastery,' said Philip, absorbed in a leaflet explaining its history.

'It's certainly a very impressive building,' said Sue as they finally left to find a good pub for lunch.

'Tim's right about the house. It's ridiculous for Mum to have four bedrooms and two reception rooms when she's living on her own. She won't sell it though, she says it's too much trouble. A four-bedroom house in London must be worth a fortune now.'

'I think I still prefer to live in Devon despite the charms and attractions of London,' said Sue.

'Me too.'

The pub started to fill rapidly as the main lunch hour got under way. It soon became clear that it was a favourite watering hole for the bright young things working in the City. Raucous laughter and animated conversation pervaded the air.

'We'd better take Mum out for a meal tomorrow,' said Philip as he returned after a lengthy wait at the bar.

'Good idea. I'll make sure I wear a pair of trousers and keep my legs covered up. I expect she'll complain they're too tight.' She let out a giggle and was pleased to see him laugh as well.

'Perhaps we can take her for an Indian meal,' said Sue.

'You must be joking she hates foreign food. We need to find somewhere more conventional, like a Harry Ramsdens.'

They went for a walk in Hyde Park and he held her hand. The relative peace was welcome after the bustle of the vibrant city streets. They sat down on a bench and watched the sparrows gather round, hoping for some lunch themselves. He kept hold of her hand. He wanted to talk to her.

'I've told the boys I'm going out with you.'

'What did they say?'

'Well, you know what boys are like at that age. They didn't say much at all. They seemed indifferent but at least they weren't hostile.'

Sue let out a nervous laugh.

'On Friday week I'm going to Taunton to bring them back for the weekend. I was wondering if you'd like to come with me.'

This time she didn't need to think too long. 'Yes, of course I'll come. It's time I got to know them better. Don't forget, I'll be working in the shop on Saturday but I can come over after work if you want me to.'

'That's great, Sue, I'm really pleased.'

'But children are not really my speciality, Philip. I've never wanted any of my own so it might not work out.'

'You say you don't want children of your own?'

'Not yet at least, but perhaps I'll feel differently in a few years' time, who knows.'

'So you'll stay Saturday night and all of Sunday with us.'

'Yes, that shouldn't be too much of an ordeal.' She started to giggle. 'I'll stay over on Friday night as well if you like.'

'That's even better.'

They resumed their walk in silence. Sue was thinking deeply. She knew she was getter in deeper but so what? It would only be for a weekend, she reasoned. For ninety per cent of the time they lived with their mother.

The week passed quickly, the lure of the capital, for a short time, infectious and rewarding. But neither of them were sad to leave or wanted to stay longer. It was a welcome break but no more than that. The train journey back to Devon was uneventful and when they arrived at Newton Abbot they found they had glorious weather to welcome them back. Philip drove out of the car park to return to Paignton, the warm sunshine making the car seem like an oven. He wound the electric windows down quickly. A mini heatwave had started with Whitsun barely two weeks away.

Clive and Matt said they were starving. The journey from Taunton had taken much longer than expected. Wailing sirens and flashing lights indicated possible trouble ahead as they approached Penn Inn at the end of the dual carriageway in Newton Abbot.

'That car is a wreck,' exclaimed Clive excitedly as they passed the scene of the accident forty minutes later.

Now that they were demanding food Sue had to rustle something up quickly. It turned out to be very tasty; spicy prawns which she had rescued from her freezer, as she didn't like them, and some cooked rice, which she had found lying idle in Peter's fridge. She mixed some frozen peas with the rice, heated the combination and, hey presto, she had cooked her first meal for the boys. She knew the prawns were very hot so she put a large jug of water on the table. Nothing was left on their plates when Sue brought in the tinned peaches and ice cream for dessert. They finished that off in double-quick time. *So far so good*, she thought, but could she keep it up for the whole weekend?

Luckily the boys were content after supper, the novelty of watching satellite television, unavailable at home, still not having worn off. The added bonus of digital television, with even more channels to explore was the icing on the cake. They went to sleep tired but happy.

'When they're a bit older they can come by train,' said Philip as Sue prepared a nightcap.

'Are you taking them anywhere tomorrow?'

'Only to the leisure centre in the morning for an hour's swimming.'

'Do you want Ovaltine or cocoa?'

'Ovaltine please. I don't suppose you'll want to come back with us to Taunton on Sunday night.'

Sue baulked at this imposition. 'No, I can't Philip, I've got a thousand things to do at home.' She saw a look of disappointment cross his face.

'You'll probably be tired by Sunday night, Sue, and I don't usually get back until nearly midnight.'

Sue wasn't too keen on the go-karting at Churston on Sunday morning but at least she only had to watch, and the weather was still perfect. She noticed that Philip didn't discipline the boys much but as they were only there for the weekend and as she was an interloper she decided not to say anything. Matt annoyingly threw the wrapper from a Mars bar on the ground without looking for a bin. Sue picked it up and looked in Philip's direction hoping that he would say something but he didn't. Still the boys enjoyed the competition on the track and burnt off some energy. They went to have lunch at the restaurant in the water park where they all had pizzas and fizzy drinks.

In the afternoon they went to Berry Head in Brixham to see the lighthouse and the Napoleonic fort. The views from the exposed headland were spectacular as they looked back to Torquay and Paignton. Sue took many photographs with her expensive camera and showed Clive and Matt how it worked. The temperature was still very high for a late spring day so Philip bought ice creams for everyone at the café by the fort.

'This wonderful weather has certainly brought the crowds out,' said Sue as they returned to the almost full main car park.

'You can see the birds nesting in the cliffs if you go into the visitors' centre,' said Philip. The boys needed no second invitation and rushed inside to see the live pictures.

Sue waited for them to leave for Taunton before she left to drive back to her flat. It had been an eventful and trying weekend but at least there had been no disasters. She found a parking space close to her flat. She hadn't had time to clean her flat for a whole week and she hated doing it in the week so this was her last opportunity. Philip and the boys would probably be close to Exeter by now. She wondered briefly if she should have gone with them but decided that no, she didn't have time and the flat badly needed a clean.

The Dyson cleaner glided effortlessly over the carpet as Sue enthusiastically got to work. Some time later she removed her clothes from the washing machine and put them in the dryer. Satisfied that the flat was sparkling clean and to her liking, she sat down with a cup of coffee and switched on the television. Tiredness suddenly crept up on her and soon she felt herself drifting off.

She woke with a sudden jolt. The telephone was ringing. She looked at her watch, it was eleven thirty. Who would be ringing at this ridiculous time? She grabbed the telephone. It was Philip.

'Something terrible has happened, Sue. Laura's dead, she's... she's taken an overdose I think. I saw a bottle next to her. The police are here. It's a complete nightmare. I don't know what to do.'

'But why, Philip?'

'I wish... I can't think straight, it's madness, she's only thirty-four. She's in the bedroom. The boys... they're in shock. So am I. I wish you were here to help.'

'Of course I'll come. Do you want me to come now?'

'Yes... no not in the middle of the night. Can you come in the morning?'

'I'll start about seven. Give me the address.'

'It's 78 Burden Street. Leave the M5 at junction twenty-six and take the A38. It's on the outskirts before you reach the town.'

'Right, Philip, I should be there by nine.'

Sue lay in bed, unable to sleep. They must be going through hell. She felt for the boys, this was a tragedy that would blight and haunt them for the rest of their lives. She felt for Philip who would have to pick up the pieces. But the thing that troubled her the most was as clear as crystal. The boys would be coming to live in Paignton. Two questions flashed before her: could she cope? And perhaps more importantly, did she want to cope?

Chapter Ten

Peter cursed as the alarm went off right by his ear. As far as he was concerned it was definitely the morning after the night before. He dragged himself out of bed and pulled back the curtains. He realised it was time to change the sheets but decided to leave it until the next day. Another boring day at work faced him and he wasn't looking forward to it. He pulled open the wardrobe and looked at his suits. Two of them badly needed a clean so he chose the dark grey one and tried to match it with a light blue and grey tie. There was just time for a hurried breakfast.

He pushed the half-empty gin bottle to one side to make more room on the kitchen table. Some stale bread was all he could find in the bread bin. He put two slices in the toaster. Half a pint of milk was left in the fridge so he could make a cup of strong tea. Stocks were sadly depleted so he realised it was an urgent priority to visit a supermarket but he knew he wouldn't have time that night, tomorrow would have to suffice. He walked into the downstairs toilet and plugged his electric razor into the socket. There was no time to do a proper job as he didn't want to be late yet again.

Sam laid the figures from head office carefully in front of Peter on his desk. He studied them with some trepidation. As he feared, they made grim reading. Sam remained standing, a solemn expression on her face.

'We're down a lot on last quarter. I didn't think it would be this bad, Sam,' said Peter.

'We are down over eight per cent, Peter.'

'That's too much, far too much. Can you sit down a minute?' said Peter.

Sam pulled out a chair from under the table and sat down opposite him. She was pencil thin, about twenty-five years old, with a pretty face, short auburn hair and a serious disposition. On her left hand she wore an expensive engagement ring. Peter had always trusted her implicitly.

'We aren't picking up much new business at the moment and we lost an important client last week,' said Sam.

'We're in July now so it's not going to be easy to put things right during the holiday weeks,' said Peter. He saw her looking at the floor. More than two years working with Sam was quite enough for him to know what that meant.

'Come on, Sam, spit it out. If you've got something to say, say it.'

'Well, do you want me to say what I really think?'

'Of course, don't pull your punches.'

'It hasn't helped with you being off sick so often during the last few months. You've seemed preoccupied lately. I assume it's because of the break-up of your marriage.'

Peter blew his top. 'My marriage has got nothing to do with anyone in this office. It's my business. Do you understand that?'

'There's no need to jump down my throat, Peter. I'm only saying what everyone else is saying.'

Peter felt his anger subside. He felt sure she was only trying to help.

'Look, Sam, I'm sorry. I didn't mean to lose my temper. I'm absolutely fine. Any problems I might have can be sorted out in no time.'

He saw her face change to a faint smile. She rose slowly and walked towards the door.

'Do you want me to get you some coffee?'

'No thanks, Sam, I'm fine for the moment.'

She closed the door quietly behind her. He immediately reached into the bottom drawer of his desk. Damn it! The bottle was nearly empty.

Peter desperately needed to be home by five. Surely they could manage without him if he left a few minutes early.

The traffic was horrendous and he used his horn to show his frustration. Johnny was waiting by the front door as Peter parked his car in front of the garage.

'Where the fucking hell have you been? I've been waiting here for over ten minutes.'

'Sorry mate, I got held up in traffic. Come inside.' Peter took off his jacket and closed the front door. Johnny, as usual, was already sitting at the kitchen table.

'How much do you want, Pete?' He laid the dried leaves out on the table. Peter took what he wanted.

'I'll pay you next time, Johnny. I haven't had time to go to the bank.'

'Okay, I believe you, thousands wouldn't,' said Johnny dubiously.

'You can trust me. I promise I'll pay you next time.'

'Okay, old mate. Do you want me to bring you anything stronger next time?'

'No, thanks. Not at the moment anyway.'

'I'd better go, I've got several more calls to make.'

Peter walked out to the front door with him. He closed the door just as Johnny drove off at speed. The little sideline to help a few mates, Peter noted, had grown into something rather more substantial.

A tin of sardines was all Peter could find for his tea. He put more stale bread in the toaster. The last scrapings from a carton of Flora margarine would have to do. The wolf, he reflected, was waiting ominously at the back door. The little piggy inside was frightened, waiting to be devoured. He planned a rescue mission the following day but he knew the financial situation was not good; funds had been left sadly depleted by the outgoings of the last few months.

He collapsed into a chair in the living room and tried to concentrate on watching a documentary on BBC2 but he found his mind wandering. Why hadn't Mandy phoned back after he had left a message with her mother? He hadn't seen or spoken to her for nearly four months. Not even a letter in all that time since she had left him. Even if the marriage was over surely they needed to talk. He wouldn't stand in her way if she wanted a divorce. He knew his behaviour had been unreasonable so what chance would he have in court anyway? He would be crucified! He kept turning the same questions over and over in his mind. Why had he been such an idiot and why didn't she contact him? He couldn't come up with satisfactory explanation and his agony was turning his life into a misery. When, he wondered, would his nightmare end? Loneliness, was also taking its toll as he spent night after night alone in his house with only the drink to keep him company.

Peter peered into the newsagent's window. A long list of advertisements appeared in the left-hand corner; anything from the sale of an unwanted pushchair to a job as a cleaner in a hotel. A small handwritten advert caught his attention – childlike in its construction and simplicity. A large round, yellow sun with rays pointing from the edges. Inside the sun was a blunt message written in blue ink, with a telephone number. Peter had a pretty good idea what 'massage' meant. He was sorely tempted. He agonised for a few moments and then felt inside his tweed jacket for his diary and a pen. He wrote down the number carefully. He swore to himself when he realised he had left his mobile phone at home and looked round for a telephone box. He saw one conveniently situated a mere twenty yards away. He walked slowly towards it searching in his pocket for loose change.

The large Victorian house must have been impressive in its prime but that was obviously some time ago. Now it had been turned into a large number of small flatlets with rubbish littering the garden. Peter only glanced at the unsavoury surroundings as he passed a rusting old car without its wheels. He searched for number ten as a large brown rat scurried across in front of him making him jump. A makeshift arrow now pointed the way up some steep narrow steps. His heart quickened as he slowly climbed the creaking stairs. She opened the door before he had time to reach the top.

Peter assessed her age as about thirty. She had a voluptuous figure and orange spiky hair, her short, tight red skirt and bikini top worn to excite.

'Hello, sunshine, was you the one who phoned a few minutes ago?'

Peter nodded apprehensively.

'What was you wanting today, love?'

'I'm not sure. How much is it?'

'It's thirty for oral and forty for sex. I need the money first.'

Peter handed over forty pounds in four crisp ten pound notes. She gave him a broad smile.

'My name's Donna, what's yours?'

'Peter,' he replied, wondering if he should have given a false name.

'Right, Peter, you can put your clothes on that chair. I'll only be a jiffy while I put the money away.'

He looked round the sad room. It was in sore need of decoration and the paint was peeling off the ceiling. The curtains were pulled tightly even though it was still broad daylight outside. Donna returned with a condom in her hand.

'Lie on your front first so I can massage your back,' ordered

Donna. Her soft hands helped him relax and he felt his desire for her increase. She put the condom on almost as soon as she asked him to turn over. Peter had sex for the first time since Mandy had left him and it was over in less than five minutes.

'You certainly needed that one,' she said, laughing as she put on her knickers. He already knew he might want to return despite the squalor of the surroundings.

'I'll do it five pounds cheaper if you come regular, Peter,' said Donna.

'Okay, I might see you again then.' He kissed her on the cheek as he said goodbye.

He scampered back to the car, anxious not to be seen, and opened the door. He felt disgusted with himself and he let his head fall back into the headrest and closed his eyes. Moments later his head jerked forward and he sat upright. Both fists came down hard onto the leather steering wheel. The impact jarred his hands and he felt tears starting to run down his face. He pulled out his handkerchief and wiped his eyes. The tears quickly dried up and his mouth felt dry. He badly needed a stiff drink. He switched the engine on and drove the two miles to his house, the gin bottle waiting to momentarily satisfy his craving.

Peter was unclear why he had been summoned to headquarters in Bristol. He had not been told much on the phone except that it was urgent. Probably, he deduced, they were going to give him a pep talk about hitting targets and ask for more effort. Still, he was confident he could weather the storm. After all, his record since landing the job of manager was impressive. Present difficulties were an unfortunate blip that would soon be rectified.

Bristol was almost a hundred miles away but once Newton Abbot had been negotiated the road was all dual carriageway and motorway. The whole journey was accomplished in a mere hour and a half. He parked his car in the spaces reserved for managers and saw that he was half an hour early for his appointment. He found a snack bar and had time for a pasty and chips.

Mr Dawkins was a thin, wiry man with a moustache aged about fifty-five. He wore an ill-fitting suit with a tie that didn't match. His companion was much younger and smartly dressed in a new suit. Mr Dawkins soon got to the heart of the matter.

'The Torquay branch was eight per cent down for the last quarter,

Mr Carpenter. The new quarter has started no better. It's the worst results in our entire network; it's not good news!'

'We should pick up in September once the holidays are over,' Peter suggested.

Mr Dawkins shook his head vigorously.

'We've been given reliable information that you have a drink problem.'

'That's not true. I've always enjoyed a drink but there's no problem. Who said there is?'

The man who was sitting next to Mr Dawkins, taking notes, looked briefly at Peter and then averted his gaze.

'Never mind that,' continued Mr Dawkins, 'we think there is a serious problem and I'm afraid we can't allow things to continue as they are at the moment. As you have obviously had some personal problems recently we are prepared to pay you for the next three months. You can, of course, see your union rep if you're unhappy. We will give you a carefully worded reference. Miss Baxter will take charge until we can find a permanent replacement.'

'Who's been putting the knife in? I want to know.'

'Several people have spoken to us, not just one person. We are going to make you redundant so there should be more money for you over and above the three months. We want to be fair to you as you've worked for us a number of years.'

'Seven years to be precise,' said Peter.

'I'm sure you'll be able to get another job once you sort yourself out,' said Mr Dawkins.

Peter could see it was a waste of time arguing as they had made their minds up. He left as soon as the formalities had been completed.

He felt a dull ache inside him. They didn't even want him to serve out his notice in the office. What had Sam and the others been saying about him? A feeling of persecution and betrayal embittered him as the stark reality of his predicament became clear. He had given many good years to that company and now they had tossed him aside like an unwanted rag doll. He trudged despondently back to his car and opened the front door. He unlocked the glove compartment and pulled out a bottle. All he needed, he calculated, was a quick swig to settle his nerves before starting on the journey back home.

'All right, Johnny, give me a little to try. We're all square now so I can pay you straight away.'

Johnny handed over a sachet of the precious white powder and put it on the table.

'That's thirty pounds, Pete.'

'I said I only wanted a little to try.'

'That's only a small amount, you idiot. You'll use that in no time.'

Peter reached into his back pocket and pulled out a wad of notes. He carefully counted out thirty pounds. Johnny grinned and stuffed them into his bulging wallet.

'Have you got a bloody job yet?'

'Not yet, but I'm looking. I'm sure I'll find something soon.'

Johnny gave a shrug of his shoulders.

'I've got to go, old mate, I'm very busy at the moment. I'll see you again in two weeks. Give me a buzz if you need anything before.'

Peter walked to the front door with him and saw Johnny's almost new gleaming dark green Audi standing impressively in the driveway. Peter kept his thoughts to himself but he couldn't help wondering how Johnny could afford it. A brief wave of the hand and the Audi sped away.

Peter's thoughts turned to more mundane matters. He badly needed to stock up on food and other essential items. He went inside to locate his keys, as a trip to the supermarket was imperative. One thing he knew was certain. The bill at the checkout would be substantial.

Peter returned an hour and a half later with the boot well filled. The bottles clinked together as he unloaded the car. As he had an important interview for a job the next day he knew it would be sensible not to start the new bottles immediately. At least the company had kept their word and given him a decent reference and he needed to make the most of that. He felt more optimistic than he had done for several weeks. He was famished so he took out a ham and mushroom pizza from one of the shopping bags and placed it in the oven. He reckoned he could polish off most of it in one go, as he hadn't had much lunch.

After supper, his palate satisfied, he went to work with a vengeance cleaning the house from top to bottom. He was feeling positive once again. The hoover, left idle for many weeks, was gainfully employed once more. Two days of dirty dishes were obliterated in one fell swoop. He sat down, feeling tired but relaxed. His new-found strength lasted only temporarily.

At around ten o'clock his mouth started to become dry. He fought it for as long as he could and resisted the temptation to open a bottle. His mind and breath needed to be clear for the interview the next morning but whatever he did he couldn't get the longing out of his mind. Biting his fingernails offered a temporary solution but the craving intensified and eventually his resistance and good intentions crumbled. Surely, he reasoned, just one drink wouldn't do much harm. He opened a whisky bottle and poured himself a very small drink. It tasted very good so he poured himself a much larger drink and left the bottle on the table beside him.

Chapter Eleven

What on earth was she going to do? Philip was clearly relying on her but Sue felt in a quandary.

'Why don't you give up your flat and come and live with us?' he had said. She knew she wasn't ready for a commitment like that and had stalled. At least the holidays were coming to an end and she would get some respite. In less than two weeks the autumn term would be commencing and the boys would be facing the challenge of starting in new schools.

Now she sat on the bed in her flat drying her hair and reliving the traumatic events of the previous two months. Clive looked to have recovered reasonably well, although he must still be hurting inside, but Matt was morose and uncommunicative. He shut himself off in his room and refused to talk to anyone, including his brother, for long periods and emerged only for meals, many of which were left untouched. The doctor had arranged counselling for both of them, but in Matt's case the results were disappointing.

The whole thing was horrendous and insoluble. As Sue struggled to untangle her hair she felt a sense of resentment that fate had conspired to treat her so badly twice within a year. How on earth did Philip think she could replace the boy's mother? It was mission impossible! On top of that she didn't even like children. The thought of taking over another woman's children was anathema to her and Philip was far too soft with them anyway. Of course they had to be treated with kid gloves immediately after the tragedy but enough was enough and now they needed more discipline. She gave a little cry of pain as she pulled too hard at her hair in frustration and threw the comb down on the bed before marching back into the living room. The clock showed a quarter to eleven. She had promised Philip she would be over at eleven so it was almost time to go.

'Where's Matthew?' asked Sue as she shut the front door and spotted Clive cleaning his shoes in the kitchen.

'Still in bed, I think.'

'Well, it's gone eleven Can you go and ask him to get up please?'

'Why don't you do it? Can't you see I'm busy?'

She let out an audible sigh.

'Where's your father?'

'In the greenhouse, I think.'

Sue opened the door to the patio and wandered down the path to the greenhouse.

'These tomatoes have come on really well, Sue,' said Philip as she opened the greenhouse door to join him inside.

'Some of them look to be ripe. We're having salad for lunch so they'll come in handy today.'

'All right, let me pick some.' He passed her six shiny red ones in a small bowl.

'I think I'll give some to the neighbours I've got far too many. I don't have much time for gardening but I do like growing tomatoes. I find it very therapeutic.'

The boys seemed to like the corned beef and jacket potatoes but were less enamoured with the tomatoes, lettuce and cucumber. Sue studied their plates with some displeasure.

'Matthew, surely you can eat more than that.'

She saw his eyes flash with anger.

'Why do you have to call me Matthew? Mum never did.'

Sue's heart sank.

'Matt that will do,' said Philip.

Sue was grateful for his support, however half-hearted and inadequate, but the damage, she knew, was done. The rest of the meal took place in an uneasy silence.

'The boys will be much more settled when they get used to their new schools,' insisted Philip as they lay naked in bed, much later, after the boys had gone to sleep.

'I hope you're right, but they won't accept me. There's a barrier there, which is going to be impossible to break down. Can't you see that?'

'Just give them time Sue, just give them time.' She turned on her side, away from him, unwilling to convey the real fears and doubts that troubled her. Soon, she knew, a decision would have to be made. How could she square the circle? How could she commit herself to a divorced man and two boys who probably despised her? Good grief, she was only twenty-eight and still very attractive so it would be easy for her to find another man. She could decide later, much later, if she wanted her own children. Peter was so weak with the boys as well. What was the point of her laying down the law if he didn't back her up? She had done as much as she could have been expected to do during the last two difficult months. Surely nobody would condemn her if she threw in the towel now and walked away.

Yet she hesitated before making the ruthless decision that logically she knew she should make. She tossed and turned as Philip slept, blissfully unaware of the crisis she was wrestling with. Sue knew it was the most important decision of her whole life. She knew that if she made the wrong choice it might come back to haunt her. Tomorrow she would ring Sally as she badly needed a shoulder to cry on. Finally, well into the small hours, she slept, her final decision postponed.

Sally was eager for Sue to visit. Bill, she said, would be out working. The expensive coffee was percolating nicely when Sue arrived. Sally's happy greeting and rapidly expanding tummy were a clear sign that her pregnancy was going well.

'Only two more months to go,' said Sally as she offered Sue a chocolate biscuit.

'I'm glad everything is fine with the baby. Is Bill shaping up well to the prospect of being a dad?'

'He's fussing around like an old hen. He's been down the library and brought back several books and he supervises my exercises.' They both laughed. 'What about you, Sue? You've got a lot on your plate at the moment.'

'You can say that again. I've got a terrible dilemma and it's driving me potty.'

'What do you mean?'

'The thing is Philip thinks it's a question of the boys getting used to me, but I can cope with that, difficult as it is sometimes. What bothers me is committing myself to them when I really want to be free. I'm getting sleepless nights, Sal, and usually I sleep like a log. I wish I knew what to do.'

'How do you feel about Philip? Would you have married him if the boys hadn't come on the scene?'

Sue sighed as her friend got to the heart of the matter. 'It was moving that way. But the boys have arrived and it's making my life impossible. They've been seriously damaged by what's happened.

Their mother's death was a terrible shock to them. I think I want him but I don't want the boys. I know I'm selfish.'

Sally rose to fetch more coffee. She filled Sue's cup but seemed to take an eternity to say anything.

'Strong-willed is how I'd put it, not selfish.'

'Thanks for that, Sal. The other night I thought about this for hours but couldn't make up my mind. I'm not usually indecisive but I still don't know what to do. Who would believe I would dither about like this? Philip will hate me if I go.'

'I don't believe that, Sue, and nor do you really. How do get on with the boys?'

'Up and down. But I can deal with that as I'm strong enough to stand up to them. That's not the real problem.'

Sally leant over and touched her softly on the hand, her face looking serious and concerned.

'I've never seen you like this before, Sue. It's a terrible decision for you to make and I feel for you, but it would be wrong for me to advise you what to do. You've got to make the decision yourself.'

'I know, but I needed someone to talk to. Thanks for listening. One thing is for certain though, I have to make a decision soon – the whole thing is driving me nuts. If I leave him I'll move out of Torbay.'

Sally looked surprised. 'I'll miss you if you do go.'

'Too much has happened in the last year, Sal, for me to stay. I've applied for jobs in London. I just want to see what's available. I should hear in the next few days.'

'The big city – that should be fun,' replied Sally.

The late summer sunshine was glorious as Sue wandered aimlessly through the St Marychurch shopping precinct still searching for answers. The summer had come and almost gone without her having time to notice. So much to deal with and so many decisions to make. *Surely*, she thought, *if I lived to be a hundred I would never have to struggle through a year like this one*. Even her mania for shopping had been emasculated by the turn of events and now she felt content to window-shop. The need to fill her wardrobe with new clothes and shoes that she would hardly wear was crushed by the sheer weight and seriousness of her problems.

She sat for a moment on a convenient seat in the pedestrianised street and surveyed the scene. The pretty flowers and bright shops made it an attractive location for holidaymakers and locals. A young, attractive blonde woman walked purposefully down the street a few yards from where she was sitting. She looked thinner in the face than when she had last seen her. Sue watched as she disappeared into a shop selling general household goods. She felt herself take in a sharp intake of breath. Sue plucked up her courage. She would try to speak to her when she came out of the shop.

'Hello, Amanda, how are you?' She saw a startled look appear on her face as she recognised who it was.

'Oh, hello, I'm fine. How are you?'

'Fine. Have you got a moment to spare? Perhaps we could sit outside and have a coffee.'

The pavement café was almost empty as they were brought their coffees.

'Do you want anything to eat?' asked Sue.

Mandy shook her head. 'You know I left Peter in February.'

'No, I didn't know.'

'We haven't spoken since. I've been ill for some time.'

'You look very well. Are you better now?'

'Yes. I've been back at work a month now. I feel so much better than I did.'

Sue was amazed how natural she was. There didn't seem to be an ounce of malice in her entire body.

'I can't help noticing you're pregnant. When's the baby due?'

'The middle of November. I don't think Peter knows.'

Sue was flabbergasted.

'Don't you think… I mean, I'm surprised you haven't told him.'

'Well, I've been depressed for so long. Now that the doctor has said I can work again I don't want anything to spoil things. My friend, Kay, says I've got to tell him but so far I haven't. I don't ever want to live with him again, you know.'

Sue felt her conscience bother her. The intense pain and humiliation of last year, a fading memory, had been overtaken by the agony of recent happenings.

'I haven't seen Peter since last October, just after you came back from your honeymoon.'

Mandy looked at her intently. 'Somebody at the bank knows where he works. He's at Nortel now. It sounds monotonous but they're doing well and the pay is supposed to be good. He lost his job at the insurance agency.'

'I wonder why that was. He had been there for years.'

'I haven't a clue.'

'Look Amanda, when I came to see you last autumn, I felt humiliated and betrayed. In fact, I could have cheerfully murdered him. Now I've got other problems to sort out. I know it's not my business but shouldn't you go and see him and tell him about the baby?'

Mandy let out a huge sigh. 'Yes I suppose so. I'll think about it.'

'Six months is a long time not to have any contact at all, Amanda.'

'Yes, sometimes it feels like only yesterday we were living together. You say you've had some problems to sort out.'

'Yeah, not half. I've been going out with somebody, it's my boss at work actually, for several months. Then out of the blue his ex-wife committed suicide after she'd been let down by her new boyfriend.'

'That's awful.'

'Worse than that, she left two boys – twelve and ten. They're living with their father now and I've had to help sort out the mess. It's been a complete nightmare.'

'I'm sorry, it sounds terrible. How have you coped?'

'Sometimes I wonder that myself but it's surprising what you can do when you have to.'

'That's very true. I wish I had been able to cope better when things went wrong,' said Mandy.

' Philip wants me to give up my flat and go and live with them in Hookhills but I don't think I can.'

'Why not?'

Sue took a sip of coffee. She wondered why she was telling Mandy all this when all she had intended to do was find out about her and Peter. But somehow she trusted the girl. 'It's very difficult for me. Firstly, how can I ever take the place of their mother? It's impossible!'

'That would be the same for any woman,' Mandy interjected.

'I know, but my problem is I don't really like children. The thought of taking over her children makes me shiver.'

Sue looked at Mandy expectantly, hoping for understanding and assistance. Mandy did not let her down.

'I'm different from you as I love children. Sometimes I wish I had trained as a nursery nurse instead of working in a bank. But I would have had a problem taking on two boys of that age so soon after their mother's death. I'm not sure I could do it. What does Philip say about it?'

'I don't think I can talk to him. He thinks it's all about me being patient and waiting for them to accept me. Men are so insensitive. He just doesn't understand at all.'

'But have you told him exactly what your fears are?'

'No, but he wouldn't understand if I did.' Sue felt alarmed that her defences had been breached and that Mandy had caught her out.

'If you need any help with the boys give me a ring.' Mandy wrote her number down on a piece of scrap paper she found in her handbag. Sue responded by handing over her business card.

'It's been lovely to see you again, Sue. I'll think about going to see Peter but it will only be to tell him about the baby,' promised Mandy as she said goodbye.

The light westerly breeze picked up and the sun disappeared behind a dark cloud as Sue walked briskly to her car. She felt cold and troubled, her mind in turmoil. Now that she knew the full extent of the havoc she had caused she felt an even stronger sense of guilt – the marriage destroyed beyond repair and a baby to be born within three months without a father. She petulantly kicked an empty drinks can towards the gutter, her annoyance growing within her. Despite what she had done the girl actually wanted to help her with the boys! She found this quite extraordinary!

Now she had to drive to Philip's house and see them all again. She opened the door of her car, feeling worn out. She couldn't go on like this otherwise she would end up in the madhouse. Sue looked long and hard at herself in the vanity mirror. She despised the face that stared back at her.

By the time she got to Philip's house she had decided to turn over a new leaf. She was determined to be as nice as pie to the boys despite any provocation that might ensue. Sue started immediately on the job of preparing the evening meal. If they turned up their noses at the delicious shepherd's pie and carrots she had patiently prepared for them she would stoically endure any taunts and brickbats that came her way. Mandy had shown her the way forward. Love and understanding would prevail. She was also prepared to put up with the disgusting amounts of tomato ketchup they covered all her food with. She hated the smell of the ketchup but she was adamant she would not say a word about it. After all, her previous ploy of trying to hide the bottle had proved to be a dismal failure anyway. It was undoubtedly time for a new start!

Today, as a treat, she decided to start them off with tomato soup and crusty rolls. This went down very well as they slurped it down noisily. She wondered if they had seen a soup spoon before as her mother had taught her a different technique to the one they were employing. Their dad, she noticed, made no comment. The next course was a bit of a disaster. Matthew unfortunately discovered a piece of gristle in his pie and subsequently painstakingly separated the potato and refused to eat any of the meat. Clive insisted that his carrots were not cooked properly and wantonly put them on the side of his plate. She smiled sweetly at him and asked if he would like to finish off with some chocolate ice cream. She was determined to look on the bright side, even after he had replied that he would have liked to have had the ice cream after his carrots had been cooked properly. It had crossed her mind that perhaps a couple of years at a boarding school might be an ideal solution for their eating habits but she managed to keep herself in check.

Magnificent Mandy had shown her the way forward. Love and understanding were the key to success. She accepted, however, that she still had some way to go as she reached inside the kitchen cupboard for some headache pills.

Philip helped her load up the dishwasher after the boys had gone upstairs to watch television.

'Are you staying the night?'

'Not tonight. I've got a lot to do at home and I've got a splitting headache.'

He kissed her lightly on the forehead.

'Matt starts at White Rock School on Tuesday. I was lucky to get him in there, as it's one of the best schools in Paignton. He can walk to school as well as it's only a few hundred yards away from home.'

'That's good news. I must fly as I've lots to do.'

'I hope you're well enough to drive.'

'Don't fuss, Philip, I'm fine. It's only a mile down the road.' She kissed him briefly on the lips and said goodnight.

She opened her front door anxious to see the post. Nothing of importance, she noted, as she tossed a couple of junk items aside. Perhaps she would do better tomorrow. She sat down exhausted. It had been a long tiring day, most of it in the shop until she had skived off an hour early to go to St Marychurch.

She decided on a luxurious, relaxing bath rather than a shower. The pills had relieved the pain but she still felt shattered. Her flat was warm and cosy as she stepped into the steaming hot bath. Again, the ramifications of her decision to apply for two jobs in London weighed heavily on her mind. She had a day owing so it would be easy to go up to London for an interview but she wouldn't tell Philip. Of course being offered a job and accepting it were two different matters. But if she was going to break off her relationship with Philip there was no way she could envisage wanting to continue working for him. It was disconcerting not to have heard anything so far but there was always tomorrow to look forward to.

After drying herself and putting on her dressing gown she made herself a bedtime drink. Although it was getting late she wanted to tidy the living room and kitchen. If she went to bed she would probably have difficulty sleeping. The same thoughts interminably wracked her brain until, sometimes, she felt the urge to cry out in the hope of ending her torment. Sure, she was fond of him but no more than that. If it hadn't been for the other problem she probably would never have gone out with him in the first place. That was it – he had caught her on the rebound. The boys were insufferable; they would ruin her life!

Her hands worked vigorously on the kitchen sink as she poured more cleaning fluid in. She wanted it to sparkle as it had never sparkled before. A cry of pain left her mouth as she caught the back of her hand on a tap, ripping a piece of skin off. The blood flowed freely as she switched on the cold water tap and let the water run over the wound. She retired to the bathroom cabinet where she found a packet of plasters and the TCP bottle standing conveniently on the same shelf. She walked to the bedroom, dabbing her eyes with a paper handkerchief. The minor injury was an irrelevance compared to what was really tormenting her.

By the time she finally slid into bed it was almost one o'clock. Her tears had now dried but her head was still spinning. She was too tired to think any more; she felt the nervous exhaustion engulf her as, for the first time in weeks, she fell asleep almost as soon as her head touched the pillow. It was almost seven hours later when she woke.

Clive and Matt arrived back home with mixed reactions to the first day at their respective new schools. Clive was enthusiastic and said he liked it. Not as good, of course, as the one back in Taunton but nevertheless he had had a good day. Matt was unable to show the same positive response to the commencement of his last year at primary school.

'How did it go?' asked his father.

'All right.'

'Who's your new teacher?'

'I can't remember her name but she's all right.'

Matt then proceeded to bury his head in a comic and, apart from a few grunts, refused to elaborate further. Sue sat in the big armchair and watched all this with only a passing interest. She hoped they would go to bed early as she needed to speak to Philip alone.

Sue fiddled with her necklace as she waited for Philip to come back downstairs. Finally, he opened the living room door and came and sat down beside her.

'Thank goodness the first day is over,' he said.

She gritted her teeth and plunged in. 'This isn't going to work out, Philip.' She closed her eyes as she saw a look of pain shoot across his face. She ploughed on, knowing her mind was made up. 'I went to London yesterday.'

'What on earth for?'

'I went for an interview. They've offered me a job. The pay's good and they want me to start in four weeks. My parents are going to lend me a deposit on a flat, assuming I can get a mortgage. The firm will arrange for me to rent a flat for a short time.'

'But I thought we—'

'So did I for a little while,' she interrupted, reading his thoughts. 'I'm not ready to settle down yet. I want to be free and I need to get away from dreary Devon.'

'It's the boys, isn't it?'

'It's not just the boys.' She felt herself grimace as she knew in her heart he was right. 'You've got a few weeks to find someone to take my place at work.' She closed her eyes again as she realised the inadequacy of what she had said.

'I'm not worried about the job, it's you I'm going to miss,' he said.

'I'm going to miss you too, but I've got to go.'

He looked heartbroken.

'Please understand, Philip.'

'I think I do. Thanks for all you've done during the last two or three months. I don't know how I would have coped without you.'

'I expect you would have coped somehow – you're quite resourceful.'

'Will you stay the night?'

She shook her head. 'I don't think that would be a good idea.'

'Perhaps you're right. What about saying goodbye to Clive and Matt?'

She studied the floor in detail until she came up with an answer.

'I think it's best if I write to them. Is that all right?'

'Yes, that's fine.'

'I'll see you in the shop tomorrow.' She walked to the door without kissing him.

Sue closed the door to her flat and went into the living room and sat down. She felt a great sense of relief now that she had finally grasped the nettle. She would write to the boys as she had promised, explaining things as best she could, but she would not go to their house again.

She felt a tingle of excitement as it suddenly dawned on her that she was about to burn her boats. Philip was a lovely man who had always been kind to her but it was time for a fresh start. She was looking forward to the challenges ahead.

Chapter Twelve

A large bill to repair the gas boiler was the last thing Peter needed. He stared, bleary-eyed, at the estimate in front of him – £240 plus VAT. The ancient boiler should really be replaced but, as he was only too well aware, he was up to his neck in debt. The balmy summer days had been replaced by the cool winds of early October. Mounting anxiety about the fragile state of the boiler led him to the inevitable conclusion that if he wanted any central heating for the winter he had to find the money from somewhere. The other envelope in front of him was his monthly credit card account. He was worried about this one. He sliced it open with his finger and looked at it with a feeling of trepidation; it was worse than he had anticipated. He looked incredulously at the top of his statement. He was only a few hundred pounds from his credit limit!

He sat down and tried to work out where all the money was going. The number and size of the direct debits could not be avoided. The mortgage bill was the largest but the others made a significant impact as well. He looked again at his credit card statement. The monthly interest payments were reaching frightening proportions. He opened the top of his desk and placed the statement carefully inside. He reckoned he could only afford to pay the minimum amount this month if he repaired the boiler. But what about the following month? He would be over the limit if he wasn't careful. Quickly he walked over to the drinks cabinet and poured himself a large one; he badly needed a stiff drink!

The golden liquid trickled down his throat, dulling his senses for a brief moment. He had been sacked from Nortel after only two weeks, which he knew would have a devastating effect on his ability to clear his debts. He desperately needed the redundancy money as he knew his basic salary would cease in only a few weeks.

Finding a clean glass in the kitchen for a drink of water was impossible so he used a dirty one. Where on earth was all the money going to? He knew the answer as soon as he asked the question. His addictions were crippling him. This week he wouldn't even have enough money to visit Donna. He knew he would have to think about selling the car and buying a much cheaper one. The Escort, despite the collapse of the second-hand car market, must still be worth several thousand pounds. He ran his hand through his unshaven face and looked out of the kitchen window. If he could find the energy he might clean the dirty windows later in the week. The garden, at the back, looked a wilderness with weeds predominating. As he wouldn't be seeing anyone today the shave could wait until tomorrow. He switched on Radio One to try to drown out his sorrows. The banal offerings from the radio soon dulled his senses and he switched it off. Tomorrow, if he felt well enough, he would wander down to the job centre and see what was on offer.

Peter had fallen asleep as the late afternoon sunshine penetrated in through the living room window. He woke with a start as the doorbell chimed. Who on earth could that be? It wouldn't be Johnny as it was only Thursday. The Jehovah's Witnesses had called the previous week and he had sent them away, so it wouldn't be them. He yawned and pulled himself out of the armchair. His slippers had disappeared so he walked to the door in his socks. He couldn't believe what he saw when he opened the door.

'Mandy! What are you doing here?'

'Hello, Peter. I was just passing and thought I'd call in and see you. Can I come in or is it a bad time?'

'No, come on in, it's nice to see you.'

He felt embarrassed, as he knew the house was a mess but he stepped aside to allow her to enter. She went straight into the living room and sat down on the settee. Peter followed her and sat down in the armchair. Suddenly she jumped up and rushed to the window forcing it open as wide as it would go. She turned round quickly, dismay written all over her face.

'Peter, it stinks in here. Don't you ever open a window?'

She marched out of the room towards the kitchen. Peter sat down to compose himself. The shock of seeing Mandy overwhelmed him. Mandy returned from the kitchen in tears.

'This place is a pigsty. What have you been doing with yourself?' She wiped her eyes with a tissue and slumped down onto the settee. Peter could hardly bear to look at her.

'Why didn't you tell me you were pregnant? Whose baby is it?'

He saw her expression change dramatically.

'It's yours, of course, Peter.'

'Why didn't you tell me if it's mine?'

He saw the anger in her eyes flare up again but she did not answer. Instead she stood up and walked out of the room to the kitchen. Peter sat with his head in his hands, feeling stunned, and incredulous. Soon he heard the sound of running water and dishes being moved. He roused himself and went out into the kitchen to see for himself what she was doing. He could see tears streaming down her face as she worked on the enormous backlog.

'I didn't ask for your help, Mandy. I can do all that myself.'

'Some of these pans will have to be soaked for ages. Please put those empty drink bottles out of my sight. Put them in the bin if you're too lazy to take them to the bottle bank.'

'I was going to clear everything up later,' he replied, pathetically. He noticed she ignored him.

'What sort of state is the house in upstairs? As if I couldn't guess.'

He decided not to offer any more feeble excuses. Much later, after she had phoned home to say she had been delayed and after he had been shamed into helping her clear up the mess, she produced a pot of tea and some sandwiches. She brought them into the living room on a tray and sat down beside him.

'I found a tin of salmon,' she said as he started eating. 'Peter, I wasn't well for several months after I went back to Mum and Dad. Now I'm fine but I don't want anything to spoil things. You can come and see the baby but that's all I want. It will be a natural birth, I hope, but I don't know if it's a boy or a girl.'

'I don't mind which,' said Peter.

'I don't mind either. The hospital says the baby is fine.'

'I lost my job at the agency. They said they had too many managers so they let me go and made me redundant. They're still paying me.'

'I heard about that. Aren't you working at Nortel?'

'Not any more. I gave it up as it didn't suit me,' he lied.

He saw her looking sternly at him.

'Peter, you're looking a terrible mess. I don't like to see you like this.'

Peter thought for a brief moment that he saw a golden opportunity.

'Mandy, couldn't we try again? I promise to make up for what has happened before.' He saw her screw up her nose.

'No! I don't want to. Look, I must go. I've been here for hours.'

'When's the baby due?'

'18 November. I hope I don't get much bigger. I'll try and call again before the birth. Please look after yourself better.'

'I've had a lot of bad luck recently. Things are sure to get better.'

'I hope so, Peter. Next time I come I'll ring you first.'

Peter sat in the dark, turning things over again and again in his mind. By his calculations she must have conceived the last time they had made love. Now he felt as flat as a pancake about the impending birth. If only it had happened earlier, as he had been hoping, she might have stayed with him. But why hadn't she mentioned a divorce? Perhaps she was saving this up until after the baby was born. He was resigned to the fact that she would probably never come back to live with him. He thought again about the birth of his child. Would he still feel as indifferent about it on 18 November? What was the use of having a baby without Mandy?

His thoughts transferred to Jim and Kay. It was ages since he had seen them. Perhaps if he spruced himself up, shaved and washed his hair, he might make himself presentable. It would be great to see them again, although he was cross they hadn't told him about the baby. He would ring them tomorrow.

He stood up and made his way to the kitchen. More than anything he needed a cold beer. He pulled one out of the fridge, hesitated briefly, and then pulled out two more. There was no point, he reasoned, in having to continually get out of his favourite armchair unnecessarily.

Peter couldn't understand what had brought about such a complete change in Kay's attitude in just three days. When he had spoken to her, on the phone, she had given him the impression that she was very pleased to hear from him. Now he was sitting petrified in her lounge and she was giving him the third degree, and, what was almost as bad, Jim was backing her up. He felt nonplussed. Now, after some preliminary skirmishing, she was getting to the reason for her irritability.

'Mandy was here two days ago and she was in floods of tears. What on earth do you think you're playing at?'

'I don't know what you're talking about.'

Kay glared straight at him. 'I'm talking about your excessive drinking, you stupid man. You must do something about it – now!'

'I haven't got a drink problem, honestly! I can stop whenever I want.'

Kay looked so angry he thought she might hit him.

'We think you have, Peter,' said Jim quietly.

'Give me a break, please. This is worse than the Spanish Inquisition.'

He saw them smile as the tension broke.

'Look, the truth is, Mandy is never going to go back to you while you're drinking like this. I helped talk her into going to see you on Thursday and what does she find when she gets there? You living in squalor and the kitchen full of empty drink bottles,' said Kay, less forcefully.

'It's true I've been drinking more recently, but I can stop whenever I want.'

Kay threw up her hands in exasperation and Jim shook his head violently.

'You need to go and see a doctor. Lots of people have a drink problem when they think they haven't. Mandy was very upset when we saw her,' said Jim.

'Mandy's never coming back to me and it's all my own fault.'

'You're right about it being all your own fault but you may not necessarily be right about her not coming back to you eventually,' replied Kay pointedly.

Peter wanted to know more. This sounded more promising.

'What makes you say that?'

'I'm her best friend. She was in deep shock after your treachery and I was very worried about her. She's fine now, or at least she was until she saw you the other day, but she's very fragile. Give her more time.'

'You said that before and look what happened.'

'I know I did. Meanwhile, Jim and I are going to monitor you and get you back on the straight and narrow, aren't we, darling?'

They both looked up to see Jim smiling in agreement.

'The first urgent task is to get you to admit you have a drink problem. Once that is done we're halfway there. Then you might have a fighting chance of getting Mandy back once you're teetotal.'

Jim looked at her in amazement. 'I never agreed to go that far,' he said laughing.

'It's going to be like in the USA. Peter is going to be on probation,' said Kay.

'Don't you mean prohibition?' said Jim helpfully.

'Ah, I expect I do. All right, Peter can be on probation and prohibition – double strength.'

Peter was finding it difficult to see the funny side. She hadn't finished with him.

'Peter, I'm deadly serious now. If you don't respond to what we're saying then our friendship is over and I'm going to wash my hands of you.'

'All right, Kay, I get the message.'

'Have you got any other skeletons in the cupboard that we should know about?'

Peter suddenly felt a bit faint. 'No, I haven't. Do you think I'm mad?'

'You'd better not have. If I find out you have you'll get a very hard kick where it hurts,' she added vehemently.

'Steady on, darling,' said Jim.

Kay stood up abruptly and marched out of the room declaring she was going to make coffee.

'Perhaps it would be a good idea to contact Alcoholics Anonymous. It can't do any harm,' said Jim.

'Perhaps you're right. I'll think about it.'

They watched the Channel Four news in silence until Kay returned with the coffee and digestive biscuits. She put the tray down on the oval glass table and invited the men to help themselves. Peter bravely put his head above the parapet again.

'I expect the baby is mine.'

He saw Kay's face change colour ominously.

'I can't believe I'm hearing this, Peter. Yes, of course, the baby is yours, you cretin. Mandy hasn't looked at another man since she met you.'

Peter wasn't quite sure what the word meant but he had a feeling it wasn't complimentary. He was crestfallen and vowed not to antagonise her further. He sipped thoughtfully on his coffee and then glanced in her direction. He could see she wanted to say something.

'She should have told you earlier about the baby. I don't know why she didn't.'

The light, intermittent drizzle came as a surprise as he drove home as most of the day had consisted of unbroken sunshine. He mulled over what had transpired. Kay had read him the Riot Act but thankfully she was unaware of his other problems. If he had told her everything he would never have left the house alive. He knew he desperately wanted Mandy back and at least she had given him some hope. Just at that moment he was full of good intentions and he suddenly felt optimistic. Perhaps, at last, he could see the light at the end of a very dark tunnel.

Chapter Thirteen

Everything in the garden appeared rosy to Sue. She had had two weeks to get used to her new job in the big city alive with sophisticated people and the happy prospect of a fat wage packet paid into her new bank account at the end of the first month. The job was new and exciting and they even said she might have the opportunity of taking photographs of well-known people. She was looking forward to that. The company, as they had promised, had arranged a flat for her to rent until she sorted out something more permanent. The flat was not pretentious but it was adequate. It had been wonderful of Philip, in the circumstances, to write her such a splendid reference to confirm her appointment. She had not written or phoned but she would always be grateful to him.

Sue liked to leave her car at home as much as possible and travel by tube and the taxis were useful if she was in a great hurry. It was almost lunchtime as she got off the Circle Line train at Westminster Station and walked to the House of Commons. She had never heard of the obscure MP she was due to photograph but apparently he represented a constituency in the industrial north of England.

It only took half an hour to complete the assignment and soon she was back outside in the chilly autumn sunshine. She remembered the nice pub where the young city types congregated which she had visited with Philip in the spring. Perhaps it would be a good place to have lunch today. She quickened her step as she realised she was feeling hungry. Would those young guys from the City still be propping up the bar as they were last time? It might be interesting to find out.

The pub was even busier this time. She found a seat at a table when a group left.

'I haven't seen you here before.' She stopped eating her pie and chips and smiled at the young man who had spoken.

'That's because I haven't been here before,' said Sue laughing. 'Well, not for a long time at least.'

He was about average height, dark and handsome but looked so very young. He put his plate of fish and chips on the table and sat down.

'You don't mind if I sit here, do you?'

'No. Why should I?'

'My name is Jeremy. I come here quite often for lunch. I work in the City for a stockbroker.'

'That sounds exciting. My name's Sue, I've only been in London a couple of weeks so this is all new to me.'

'I knew I hadn't seen you in here before. Who could forget someone as good-looking as you?'

She finished her pie and chips and sat watching him eat.

'Do you want another drink?' asked Sue.

He raised his eyebrows and glanced at her.

'Well, er, I suppose so if you're going to the bar. I'm driving so just a half of best bitter please.'

She returned shortly with the bitter and a lager and lime for herself. She watched him finish off the fish and chips.

'I expect you usually plaster that with tomato ketchup,' said Sue.

A frown appeared on his forehead. 'Tomato ketchup? I hate that muck! I wouldn't contaminate my food with that stuff.'

Sue smiled at him. She wanted to make sure she had her priorities sorted out right from the start.

He took her to a West End show in his new sports car. They saw *The Witches of Eastwick* at the Drury Lane Theatre Royal. Sue noticed he had plenty of money to throw in her direction and plied her with drinks throughout the evening. He had already presented her with a large box of chocolates when he had picked her up at the flat. Later he made love to her in his large, spacious, luxurious house. When she woke the next morning Jeremy was already wide awake. He saw no reason at all why she needed to complete the deal on buying her new flat in Finchley.

'Move in with me, honey,' he urged.

She considered the offer seriously as it had its attractions. She could see he was brash with a clear awareness of his own importance but she liked the confident air he showed about everything he did. She weighed up the pros and cons. He was a year younger than she was but that was nothing. The mortgage payments would take a hefty slice of her income. He was quite good as a lover, although a bit selfish.

Perhaps he was worth a gamble.

'Well, it would save a lot of trouble and expense if I did.'

'Right, it's agreed then. You move into here in two weeks when the rent runs out on your flat. Or you can move in before if you like. The sooner the better I say.'

Sue's face broke into a broad grin. 'Okay, I'll move in as soon as I can get my stuff over here.'

'Great. I've got a mate who can help you with that. Give him a few quid and he'll be happy. He's got a large van.'

Sue felt excited about the decisiveness of her new lover. The agonising trials and tribulations of the last year were, hopefully, put firmly behind her. This was an exciting start and a perfect opportunity to rebuild her life with the painful memories of hurt and indecision consigned to the waste bin. She had eagerly grasped the chance offered to her and there was no point in looking back.

Jeremy jumped out of bed and started dressing. Sue stayed where she was and watched him.

'I've been invited to a party next week, Sue. Can you wear something sexy, it's sure to be great fun.'

Sue liked parties but hadn't been to one for so long. She was sure she could find something suitable for this one.

Sue wore a sleek low cut dress to the party and Jeremy gave her an approving wolf whistle when he saw her in it. He left his car and home and they made the short journey by taxi, which made them a little late. He urged the driver on from the back seat, which made Sue laugh and eventually they arrived.

Jeremy's shock of dark brown hair made him look even younger than twenty-seven. His dark expensive suit and matching tie attracted admiring glances from many of the glamorous young women present. Sue, still a novice at such gatherings, did not feel out of place and was soon enjoying herself. Jeremy was attentive and supplied her with drinks at regular intervals and the fun and laughter continued unabated.

'You seem to know lots of people here, Jeremy,' she said in a rare quiet moment.

'Yeah, I get a lot of invites to these sort of bashes. If you stick with me you won't go far wrong.'

She saw him finish off another martini in double-quick time and call loudly for another one. As the music got slower and more romantic so Sue's escort became more volatile and the worse for wear. Later she had to help him into a taxi. Still, she thought, as they journeyed home with Jeremy's head resting on her shoulder, she had had a few drinks as well. In fact she felt positively light-headed as she saw him doze off. She woke him as they reached their house. They zigzagged their way to the front door with the young taxi driver offering his assistance. Eventually Sue managed to insert the key in the lock and they staggered inside.

Sue was getting worried as she hadn't seen him like this before. She tried to give him some strong black coffee but he was having none of it. His drunken amorous advances bewildered her as he grabbed hold of her arms and held them firmly by her side, kissing her urgently on the mouth. He held her in a vice-like grip as she struggled to break free and they toppled backwards onto the bed. She could feel his hands reaching under her dress and clawing at her knickers. She fought against him and cried out in pain.

'Jeremy, you're hurting me. Please stop!'

He carried on regardless and she decided it was best not to resist. He lay on top of her and she felt a sharp pain as he entered her. Her ordeal was short and soon he rolled away and lay in a drunken stupor on the bed next to her. Sue fled to the bathroom in tears and locked the door. Gently she slid down onto the floor, by the door, and cried her eyes out.

In the morning he was full of remorse.

'I'm sorry about what happened last night, Sue. It won't happen again. I had too much to drink,' he said as they lay in bed.

'That's no excuse, Jeremy. You were very rough and you hurt me. I'm bruised and very sore.'

She was in a quandary as she had nowhere else to go. Did the apology mean anything? She had her doubts but should she give him one more chance? He turned towards her and she could smell the drink on his breath.

'Why don't we go off for a week next month? I can easily afford it. I've always fancied going to Hawaii. The beaches are supposed to be fabulous. What do you say?'

She felt humiliated but decided not to reject the offer out of hand.

'I'm not sure I can take a week off as I've only just started my new job.'

'We could go at Christmas if you like. Yes, that would be better and we could stay longer. Remember I'm paying, so you think about it.'

'Okay, I'll think about it. Hawaii sounds very exotic.'

'Yeah, it will be great. I'm sure we'd have a ball.'

'Where are you going today, Jeremy?'

'White Hart Lane. Spurs are at home this week.'

'Do you go often?'

'Every home game – I've got a season ticket.'

'I went to see Torquay once and I almost died of boredom.'

Jeremy laughed. 'This is a bit different from Torquay. The ground holds 35,000 people and it's packed every match. And that's with the team playing rubbish away from White Hart Lane. I should be back about six.'

Sue got out of bed and made for the bathroom. She fancied a holiday in Hawaii. The physical and mental pain was still vivid in her memory but perhaps he was worth one more chance. But what she regretted, more than anything, was not taking the opportunity to buy her own flat. Now she was living with a man she no longer trusted. What an impetuous fool she had been!

It turned out to be a good compromise. They would leave Heathrow on Boxing Day bound for Honolulu International Airport on the island of Oahu. That way Sue wouldn't have to take any time off work. Ten days in this Pacific paradise, with the debonair Jeremy footing the bill, now looked increasingly attractive. Sue sat glued to a *Lonely Planet* guide to the Hawaiian Islands. It sounded breathtaking! And what was this about the Ala Moana Centre in Honolulu itself with almost two hundred shops: Sears, Liberty House and many other department stores? The mind boggled, she could have a field day here. Yes, Hawaii obviously had additional plusses over and above what she had originally envisaged.

'As we are there for ten days we ought to visit at least one of the other islands,' said Sue as they relaxed together looking at the guide.

'We could fly to the Big Island and spend a couple of days there. It should be interesting and I can afford it, no problem.'

'Good, I'm glad you're so flush, Jeremy.'

'Right, that's finalised then, we'll book a hotel for a week on Oahu and then go to the Big Island for two days. The guide says there's plenty of accommodation even at Christmas time. What do you think, pal?'

'I agree with everything you say, Jeremy.'

Sue's anticipation of a holiday to be remembered was increasing by the minute. She turned her attention to the travel arrangements once they were there.

'It seems the best way to travel round Oahu is by bus unless, of course, we hire a car,' said Sue.

'Yeah, let's hire a car,' said Jeremy impetuously.

'This holiday is going to be very expensive,' countered Sue.

'You haven't seen the size of my Christmas bonus, honey, it's going to be enormous. As I've told you before, Sue, stick with me and you won't go far wrong.' He let out a loud laugh.

Sue responded with a giggle. She had got over the initial shock of his violence to her and there had been no repeat occurrence. Now she felt hypnotised by the affluence that surrounded him. He seemed oblivious to the trials and tribulations that affected lesser mortals as he was determined to live life to the full. Ruthless was the word that came to Sue's mind but, so what, she needed this holiday. She was sure she deserved it after all she had had to endure recently. Clinging on to this young mans shirt tails, at least for the moment, suited her down to the ground.

The hotel was luxurious and modern and the views over the white sand beach stunning. The weather was less promising with showers threatened, but the temperature was still high and the water looked inviting with the sea calm. They resisted the temptation to try the water and instead took a taxi to Chinatown.

'It's just like being in Asia,' said Sue, excitedly, as yet another restaurant came into view.

'Do you want to try a Chinese, Vietnamese, Thai or Filipino restaurant?' asked Jeremy.

They settled for a Vietnamese restaurant in River Street. Apparently the speciality was a thick soup called 'pho' which turned out to be delicious. Beef broth with rice noodles and thin slices of beef garnished with cilantro and green onion. A second plate of fresh basil, bean sprouts and slices of hot chilli completed the feast.

'I really like Chinatown, we must spend more time here,' said Sue as they left.

They wandered through the colourful streets for some time until they finally came to rest at a convenient bar. The place was packed with Americans and Japanese. It took a long time to be served but

Jeremy finally made it back.

'I want to visit Pearl Harbor while we're here,' said Jeremy as he handed Sue her fizzy drink.

She bided her time, as she wanted the beaches and the shops. It was imperative, she decided, that she made the most of those exquisite white sandy beaches. Tomorrow couldn't come soon enough.

Sue and Jeremy were down at the Ala Moana Beach early the next morning. The sandy beach looked as if it went on for ever and the water was warm and inviting.

'I'm going for a swim. Are you coming?' asked Jeremy.

'No, I want to stay here and get a nice suntan.' Sue watched as he ran headlong into the clear blue sea and immediately swam off at a fast crawl. She removed her bikini top and applied a liberal amount of sun lotion. The sun was already strong with the temperature in the seventies. She had the day meticulously planned. The morning dedicated to the beach and then a leisurely stroll to find a nice bar for some salad for lunch. Then, most importantly, a full assault on these two hundred shops situated just a couple of minutes away. What bliss!

She was lying on her back, with her eyes closed when he returned.

'Put your top back on, Sue. I don't like men looking at you.'

She put her hands to her breasts and sat upright. 'Why not? Lots of the girls are topless.'

'Put it back on. I don't like it.'

He lobbed the offending object in her direction and it landed on her navel and she hastily put it back on.

'I don't know why you're making so much fuss,' said Sue.

He ignored her. 'The water was warm. I had a great swim.'

He reached for a towel and started to dry himself. She gazed in admiration at his lithe, taut body as he lay down beside her on a lounger. His dark hair was still soaking wet. She passed him another towel.

'I think I'll just have a quick look round the shops across the road after lunch,' she announced casually.

Jeremy carried on vigorously rubbing his hair with apparent disinterest. She was determined not to be thwarted this time. Losing the battle of the bikini top was very unfortunate. Not visiting the alluring shops unthinkable.

'Are you coming with me?'

'Well, we can't stay in the sun all day. It's too bloody hot already.'

'I assume that means yes.'

'Yeah, okay, for a little while. I need to buy a couple of T-shirts for the beach. What do you want?'

'I just want to browse and see what they're selling.'

Sue moved over on to her front and unzipped her bikini top. The second round was hers on points but she still felt uneasy about the bikini top incident. She dozed off to the sound of the lapping waves in her ears as they edged ever closer with the tide coming slowly in.

The fat wallets of the Americans and Japanese were very much in evidence as the stores reverberated to the sounds of the hordes of tourists enticed from the other islands to the main shopping centre. The continually ringing tills were a delight to the store managers. Jeremy found some nice shirts and purchased two. Sue was astonished at her self-restraint. She still enjoyed looking, and she bought a couple of brightly coloured dresses, but the urgent need to buy and buy was less pressing than before. Perhaps, she thought, she was becoming more responsible as she grew older.

Jeremy was more than happy to spend as much money as possible, so in the evening they chose a Chinese restaurant in the heart of Chinatown on the pedestrian mall. They picked plates of seafood from the extensive menu.

'We'd better hire a car early if we're going to drive round the island tomorrow,' said Jeremy as they waited for the food to arrive.

'By my calculations it's about a hundred miles round the island. Do you want me to do some of the driving?' She saw him screw up his nose in disgust.

'No thanks, honey, you leave the driving to me.'

She felt hurt and resentful but decided to keep her mouth shut. The food arrived and the portions were enormous!

'Let's try the local brew,' said Jeremy, without consulting her.

It had a strong taste and was very bitter. Sue couldn't drink it and asked for something sweeter. It was late when the taxi dropped them back at their hotel. In bed they made love passionately for a long time. He was a strong lover but Sue wished he would think more of her needs rather than just his own.

Long after he had tired himself out and gone to sleep Sue lay in bed thinking. Peter had been the only man who had ever completely satisfied her sexually. Her hatred of him was a fading memory now that she had engineered a revenge that horrified even her. Had he found someone else, she wondered. Mandy would never go back to him. She recalled how tender and considerate his lovemaking had been and how, despite a succession of lovers, she still missed it. She remembered how they had completely satisfied each other's sexual needs. For the first time in several months she remembered she would have jumped at the opportunity to marry him if he had asked her. Then had come the terrible humiliation and shock that enveloped her when she discovered the awful truth. The last time she had seen him she had contemptuously slammed the door in his face. *Time*, she thought, *is a great healer*. Now, over a year later, she knew she didn't feel quite the same way.

Naturally Jeremy insisted on hiring a large car. Sue wasn't paying so she let him get on with it.

'It's automatic,' said Jeremy looking pleased with himself. He decided, after consulting a map, to tackle the island anti-clockwise. Sue had to admit the car was very smooth and comfortable. The southeast of Oahu turned out to be a treasure trove of beautiful scenery as they travelled along the coastal road. Inland they could see the dominant Koolau Mountains. On the seaward side they saw lovely coastal views and, adjacent to the road, volcanic craters and lava sea cliffs.

As they proceeded north along the eastern coast road, the Koolau Range protruded outwards almost as far as the sea. They stopped for lunch at one of the pleasant beaches. The beach was very flat with golden sands.

'This place is ideal for swimming. I'm going for a quick dip,' said Jeremy.

He soon disappeared out of sight as he ran into the water and swam strongly away. Sue took the opportunity to indulge in a spot of furtive topless sunbathing. Her bikini top kept close by for when he reappeared on the horizon. Jeremy returned invigorated. Sue sat on a towel looking decorous, her top demurely in place.

'That was great,' announced, Jeremy as he excitedly shook his hair, spraying her with icy cold water. She howled her derision at him and smartly withdrew to a safer distance clutching her towel.

'You should have come in, Sue. It was really smashing.'

'I hate the water – I can't even swim.'

'Really? I'm surprised about that. Come on, we need to get a move on.'

Jeremy was already sitting in the driver's seat, impatiently tapping his fingers on the steering wheel when Sue put her head in though the window.

'I think you've got a flat.'

'A flat what?'

'A flat tyre, Jeremy. Your precious car has got a flat tyre.'

He looked at her as if she was something from outer space.

'I don't believe it.'

'Well, come and look for yourself.'

He clambered out of the car, brushing her aside, and rushed to inspect the problem. Seeing the lack of air in the tyre he kicked it, made a critical remark about the firm that had hired him the vehicle and opened the boot to look for the spare tyre and a jack.

'Are you going to ask for a refund?' asked Sue.

After some swearing and sweating the spare wheel was eventually put on. Sue thoughtfully handed Jeremy a Coca Cola as he sat on the ground wiping the perspiration from his brow with his hands and shirt front covered in grimy oil stains.

'As soon as I clean up we'll get going.'

The Oahu North Shore was something they both wanted to see. The huge winter waves were ideal for the surfers. They watched in awe as enormous waves swept in from the erupting sea. They stopped to catch their breath at a small restaurant.

'The surfing is always better in winter as the waves are much bigger,' said the waitress.

Jeremy, this time with Sue's approval, ordered shave ice with ice cream. The sweet syrups and ice delicious with the chocolate and vanilla ice cream.

'The coastline of this island is superb. Jeremy. It's a pity we don't have time to cross from east to west and travel through the mountains.'

That was about it! The Waianae Coast, the western coast was dull and uninviting. Unlike the rest of the island it had not been developed for the tourists. They completed the last lap of their adventure without stopping and were back in Honolulu in time for supper in Chinatown. The new year was only a few hours away.

Sue was mighty glad to see the back of the old year. As they touched glasses and toasted in the new one she fervently hoped it would be a big improvement on the last one. Chinatown, as the magic hour approached, had been a hive of activity. Fire-eating dragons and colourful costumes had added to the excitement. As they returned to their hotel Sue felt that the new year had got off to a promising start. Jeremy was boisterous but thankfully not inebriated. Sue was feeling optimistic and cheerful even though the new year was only one hour old.

'We won't be able to drive round the Big Island, that's for certain, it's ninety-three miles by seventy-six,' said Jeremy as their plane circled Kona Airport waiting to land.

'Let's stay close to Kona, that's the main tourist area anyway,' suggested Sue.

Safely ensconced in a comfortable medium-sized hotel they took advantage of the sunny weather and went to the beach. Jeremy cleared off to rent some snorkel gear while Sue lounged on the beach sun-bathing. The temperature, even though it was winter, rose into the eighties. Her body was now a satisfactory deep brown colour. Sue wished they could have stayed longer. Jeremy had come up trumps but she still didn't trust him completely. London would inevitably be cold and damp in January but Jeremy's house, in the affluent part of Islington, was an impressive residence. She decided it would be wise to sit tight and see how things developed. The holiday had been a welcome and much needed break but very soon it would be back to the real world.

Sue was a bit miffed that Jeremy had been preoccupied the night before and she hadn't seen him at breakfast either. By the time she had surfaced he had left long ago for the City. Now, unexpectedly, she had most of the afternoon to herself. She was pleased she had left the car at home as it was a nice day and she needed the exercise. Perhaps she should find a gym and work out once a week. She embarked from the tube train and walked briskly to Jeremy's house just six hundred yards away. The weather was clear and cold and she quickened her pace to keep warm. She hadn't fully embraced Islington, which she thought to be a strange mixture of pockets of great wealth but made up predominately of massive council estates. She knew that many of the residents lived in grinding poverty and she felt uneasy about this.

Sue was anxious to get back as soon as possible to do some cleaning and spruce the house up. She turned the corner and the large, imposing detached house came into view. What on earth was Jeremy's car doing there at this time of day? She was certain he had taken it to work earlier in the day! As she got closer she saw that the curtains to their bedroom were tightly drawn. She felt her heart beating wildly as she approached the front door. She turned the key as softly as she could and pushed the door gently. It opened just enough for her to squeeze inside without the door squeaking. She closed the door as quietly as she could.

The house was silent. Perhaps he was ill in bed. That would explain the deathly silence. Perhaps something more sinister was going on; that would explain the silence as well. She mounted the stairs slowly, hoping the thick carpet would cushion her footsteps and at the top she could see that the bedroom door was closed. Sue wondered if she had the courage to open it. She stood, transfixed, outside the door terrified of what she might find inside. She put her ear to the door and listened. This time she heard the unmistakable sounds of heavy breathing and she felt the anger building up inside her. She looked at the door handle in front of her and agonised about whether she could do it. She used all her courage, turned the handle and pushed the door open. A shrill female scream greeted her as she saw two naked bodies intertwined on top of the bed. She slammed the door shut and fled downstairs to the living room.

Within a couple of minutes she heard the bedroom door open and footsteps rushing hurriedly down the stairs.

'Take the keys, Jo, and go and wait for me in the car,' she heard him say.

The living room door burst open and Jeremy strode in, looking dishevelled and flushed. Sue didn't know where to look.

'You never come back at this time of day,' he yelled accusingly.

She felt her blood boiling. 'Me! Are you blaming me for coming back early. How long has this been going on? Did I spoil your fun?'

She stood up and walked towards him. Their eyes met in the centre of the room and she saw a mocking smile cross his face.

'If you don't like the present arrangements you know what you can do.'

'Did you have to do it in our bed? You bastard!' She saw his face turn to anger.

'You bitch. I've spent a lot of money on you.'

'Well, you won't have to worry about that—'

She didn't see the blow coming. His open hand struck her full on the side of the face and she reeled back, clutching her cheek and landed in an undignified position, sitting on her bottom, near the settee. The shock and pain rendered her speechless as Jeremy turned away and stormed out, slamming the door behind him. She heard the car rev up loudly and speed away. Sue dissolved into tears, her pride, as much as anything, injured by the unexpected violence. She hauled herself upright and rushed into the downstairs toilet. Her face felt numb from the sickening blow and she peered anxiously into the mirror for any signs of physical damage. She was relieved that there was no obvious bruising.

Her brain had already gone into overdrive. Perhaps, Pat, her friend from work could put her up for a few days. She and her husband, Guy, had a spare room. She couldn't stay where she was, that was unthinkable. She dialled immediately.

'I've got to leave today, Pat. He hit me! Can you be an angel and help me out? It would only be for a day or two.'

'Are you all right, Sue?'

'Yes, don't worry about that, I'm fine. But I can't stay another night in this house. Please can you help me?'

'Of course we can. How long will it take for you to get to our house?'

'I don't know. I've got quite a lot to pack. Probably about two hours but I might have to make two journeys.'

'Okay, I've got an idea. I'll leave work early and bring my car over to you. I can probably get off in about half an hour. Give me your address and I'll be over as soon as I can.'

Sue put the phone down and took a moment to assess the situation. She was amazed how clear and certain her thoughts were. A few tears had been shed but now she felt confident she knew exactly what to do. No man had ever hit her before and Jeremy was not going to hit her again!

Pat arrived just as she had finished squeezing the last of her dresses into the back seat. Sue was very relieved.

'Thanks for coming, Pat. I've got two more suitcases. Can they go in your boot?' She hoped and prayed they could complete the task before he came back. There was a last minute inspection to make sure she hadn't missed anything.

'That's it, Pat. I think I've got everything. Let's make a run for it.'

She left her front door key on the living room table together with a cryptic note saying how much she had enjoyed his generosity. But now, as she explained, it was time to leave and look for greener pastures. She slammed the door behind her and saw Pat already had her engine running.

'This reminds me a bit of James Bond,' said Pat, smiling.

'Which film were you thinking of in particular?' said Sue, grinning back at her.

'The one where he escapes and then blows the house up,' said Pat.

'I don't think I'll blow his house up, although he probably deserves it,' said Sue.

They drove away without a backward glance. If Jo wanted to move in and take her place she wished her the best of luck. Poor girl! She was certainly going to need it.

Now that Sue had been staying with Pat and Guy for a week the stark reality of her predicament was very clear and was starting to prey on her mind. The initial euphoria of a new job in London was inevitably starting to fade. She missed her family and friends in Devon and she stayed awake long into the night wondering what to do. When she woke in the morning the decision hit her straight away but she wanted to talk to Pat first.

'I think I'm going to give a month's notice tomorrow,' said Sue as she made coffee in Pat's kitchen, late the following evening.

'I thought you were enjoying the job,' replied Pat.

'Yeah, I am, but now I've got nowhere to live and my city boyfriend turned out to be a disaster. My father's health is deteriorating and my family would like me to come back to Devon and I miss my friends back home. I want to go back and live in Tavistock. I'm sure I can get a good job in Plymouth.'

'Why did you come to London?'

'It would take a week to explain but I can probably sum it up in one word – men. About a year and a half ago I'd been going out with this guy for about a year and he wanted to marry me but I dropped him. Since then it's been downhill all the way. Now I come up to London and find the same problem – men.'

'I have noticed you do attract men,' said Pat, laughing.

Sue ignored her and let out a heavy sigh. 'I don't know why everything has gone wrong.'

'You can stay here for the next month if you're going home. Guy won't mind.'

Sue's eyes lit up. 'Can I? That would be super. Your husband is really sweet.'

'We have our ups and downs. I'd like to give up work and have a baby but Guy says we can't afford it. We earn about the same so he may be right. Teachers don't get very well paid, you know. Shall we take our coffee into the lounge?'

They both sat down on the sofa and Sue found herself becoming sad.

'Sometimes I think I'm abnormal not wanting kids,' said Sue, mournfully. Pat's large ginger tomcat, Lucky, jumped on to her lap and started to purr loudly. Sue stroked him along his back and then with her forefinger under his chin. He soon curled up into a contented ball. 'In the next life I might prefer to be a cat.'

'Don't tell me you believe in reincarnation,' said Pat.

'Not really but domestic cats do have an easy life. This one is so fat and healthy.'

'Guy and I go to church most Sundays. We go to the Methodist church about a mile from here.'

'I don't think God would will be very impressed with some of the things I've done in my life, Pat, I hardly ever go inside a church.'

'You should try it. God is very forgiving.'

Sue felt tears welling up in her eyes. 'I did something awful just over a year ago. I don't want to talk about it but I feel so ashamed.'

'Sometimes it's good to talk about things you've done in the past and feel bad about.'

Sue touched her eyes with a tissue. 'Something horrible happened to me and I took my revenge but, looking back, it may have been partly my fault. Let's talk about something else.'

'Okay, but you're welcome to come to church with us on Sunday if you think it would help.'

'Thanks Pat, I'll think about it.'

'Men can be so difficult. Guy and I fight like cats and dogs at times.'

'Don't I know it; men are impossible at times.'

'Don't tell me you don't like men.'

Sue let out a giggle. 'I like men, of course I do. The problem is they don't always do what I want them to do.'

Pat laughed.

'When I get back home perhaps I'll meet someone handsome, sexy and nice. It would be a bonus if he's rich as well.'

They both roared with laughter. Guy, intrigued by all the commotion and merriment, poked his head round the door.

'Not laughing at me, I hope.'

'No, love, just men in general. You're all impossible.'

Sue yawned. 'I think I'll turn in now. See you both in the morning.'

Sue lay in bed daydreaming. She was definitely leaving in a month. The great London adventure would have lasted a mere four and a half months and she had set out with such high hopes. She would tell her boss she needed to go back home to help look after her ailing father. London had been a wonderful experience and most of it had been fun. But it was almost over and very soon it would be time to go back to her roots.

Chapter Fourteen

The redundancy payment had arrived in the nick of time and Peter's head was still above water, at least for the next few weeks anyway. But the debt he had accumulated had reached frightening proportions. A much needed job, albeit a low paid one, had materialised on the Yalberton Industrial Estate and that had done wonders for his self-esteem. Two hundred pounds a week was better than nothing but he was only too well aware that there was far more going out than coming in. He was becoming desperate. He decided it would be sensible to go and see someone at the Citizens Advice Bureau as he badly needed help and advice. They made an appointment for him to see one of the trained volunteers.

He arrived wearing his best suit and feeling nervous. Kathy was friendly and helpful. She was middle-aged, with untidy, medium-length auburn hair and a plump rounded face. Her glasses kept slipping down her nose as she got to work trying to sort Peter out.

'We used to have a unit dedicated to helping people overcome debt, but cutbacks mean we can only give general advice now. Debt is a very common problem, you know. At least you have come to us earlier than most people do.'

'I don't want to sell the house unless I have to.'

'You may have to sell it but hopefully that can be avoided. Renting is very expensive as well.'

'It's dead money,' said Peter.

'Quite. You say you have started to go to Alcoholics Anonymous.'

'Yeah, I started going about three weeks ago. Drinking was costing me a fortune.'

'But you now have a job so that should help you as well.'

'I'm worried about the mortgage repayments.'

'You need to write to your mortgage provider and explain that you may have difficulty in meeting the repayments. They might be helpful. It's best to do that before you miss a monthly repayment.'

Peter nodded sagely. He wanted to make a good impression.

'You need to make a careful list so you can see exactly how much is going out each month and then match it as far as possible with your income. Then stick to your plan. Are there any other areas where money is leaking?'

Peter averted his eyes. Surely he didn't need to tell her all the sordid details.

'No, I think I've told you everything.' He felt beads of sweat starting to accumulate on his face. 'I think I need to take my jacket off, it's hot in here.'

'You live on your own, do you, Mr Carpenter?'

'Yeah, that's right. I'm married but we're separated.'

Kathy nodded sympathetically.

'The most important thing with debt is to have the will to sort the problem out. Once you have produced a plan to reduce the money you owe you must stick to it. I hope you have got that will.'

'Yeah, I think I have. I've never been in debt before.'

'Come and see us again if you need to. Try and keep the house if you possibly can. At least it must be worth a lot more than the mortgage. Good luck!'

The watery pale November sun was very low in the sky as he emerged from his ordeal. He felt humiliated but the thought of getting Mandy back was the driving force behind his desperation. If he lost the house that would be another nail in his coffin. He reached his car. He knew he should have sold it weeks ago and now the financial situation was so critical he would have to sell it immediately. Perhaps he could get a good part exchange deal from a dealer and buy a much cheaper car. His gloom deepened. He needed solace. Perhaps the crack he still had at home would do the trick but supplies were running low. Thank goodness Johnny would be arriving tomorrow to replenish stocks.

As 18 November approached Peter found himself becoming anxious. They would ring him, they said, as soon as there was any news. He had decided he wanted a daughter. Perhaps she would look like Mandy.

Kay rang him at one in the morning on the nineteenth. She sounded cool, calm and collected.

'You have a beautiful, bouncing baby daughter. She weighs seven and a half pounds. She looks a bit like you.'

'That's great! Is Mandy okay?'

'She's fine but a bit tired. The birth went very smoothly. Do you want to come over?'

Peter was out of the traps like a startled hare. He didn't feel his best but he dressed in record time. He raced to the front door and skidded to a halt. The flowers! He had almost forgotten the flowers. They were in a vase in the living room and he had some paper to wrap them in as well. He saw they were drooping a little but it was the thought that counted, and he wasn't to know the baby wouldn't be early.

The journey to the Maternity Department of Torbay Hospital was not completed entirely within the required speed restrictions. He shouted into the intercom that he had arrived but they seemed to take an age to let him in. Finally, they relented and the door opened. A pretty nurse smiled at him and showed him the way.

The baby was as quiet as a little mouse as Mandy handed the little bundle to Peter to hold. He looked at his tiny daughter, her blue eyes staring straight up at him. His eyes turned away to look at Mandy. Her face was flushed with success and pride, her grin as wide as a house.

'Thanks for the flowers, Peter. They're nice,' said Mandy.

'She's absolutely lovely,' said Peter as his eyes misted up. He suddenly felt a great sense of achievement as he carefully handed her back to Mandy. Kay produced a cup of tea to calm him down.

'We both think she looks a lot like you,' said Kay.

'Do you think so? Have you decided on a name?' asked Peter.

'I want to call her Louise. Is that all right with you?' asked Mandy.

'Yeah, Louise is a nice name. I think that's great.'

'Good, then Louise it is. Do you want to hold her again?'

Peter took her in his arms and made a face at her. She closed her eyes and went to sleep and Peter rocked her gently, to and fro. Eventually a nurse took her and he sat down on the bed.

'How long do you think they'll keep you in for?' asked Peter.

'I expect I'll be home in a couple of days, they don't keep you in long these days.'

He looked up to see Kay putting the flowers close to Mandy. He wondered if she really liked them. Perhaps she had more important things on her mind.

He drove home feeling exhilarated but also resentful. Why hadn't he been there at the birth like all the other fathers? He wished that Mandy and Louise were coming back to his house. This, he conceded, was all his own fault but nevertheless he had hoped for a miracle. Sadly a miracle had not happened and now he was going home to an empty house and a mountain of debt.

Peter was determined to stay off the drink and two weeks had gone by without him touching a drop. The crack cocaine was different, he badly needed that even though it was costing him more than the drink ever did. One thing at a time, he decided. He would deal with the crack problem once he had conquered his drink addiction. He was certain he was now on the right road and at last sorting his life out. The ultimate prize was elusive but perhaps not completely out of reach. The baby had heightened his desire to save himself and Mandy and Louise were the motivation for his rehabilitation. He would be seeing them every two weeks. This, he knew, would be torture but the alternative too horrible even to contemplate.

Johnny arrived as usual, almost on time. He seemed to have his round on a very tight timetable. He was always glancing at his expensive watch to make sure he had not fallen behind.

'Are you sure you don't want to try some heroin, Pete? There's nothing quite like it for a great feeling, mate.' said Johnny persuasively.

'No, I bloody well don't,' replied Peter decisively.

'Well, if you do, just let me know. How much crack do you want?'

Peter picked up a medium-sized bag. He counted out £50 and handed the money over. Johnny pocketed the notes with a satisfied look on his face.

'See you in two weeks, Pete. Think about the heroin. I'm never short and I always sell the best quality stuff.'

Peter felt a feeling of revulsion but realised he couldn't afford to bite the hand that fed him. However, he knew, whatever else happened, he must resist getting hooked on anything else.

'See you in two weeks, Johnny,' he replied meekly at the front door. The car was gone in an instant.

With Kay and Jim coming round to spy on him he knew he had to make a big effort to get the house in some kind of order. If they found out he was taking drugs he would be ostracised and his life would not be worth living. Thankfully, they were blissfully unaware and all they could see was that he was winning his battle with the considerable help of Alcoholics Anonymous against the demon drink. He produced cups of coffee and hot cross buns as soon as they arrived.

He smiled as Kay looked suitably impressed. He knew that if she even suspected the truth he was dead meat.

'You seem to be winning the drink battle,' said Kay.

Peter sensed the time was right to exploit the situation. 'Have one of these buns, Kay.'

She took one and started eating.

'Yes, I am getting back on the straight and narrow. Probably I could have given up on my own but the sessions aren't too painful and it's nice to be able to help other people. We all help one another.'

'Remember, you'll never be free from this for the rest of your life,' said Kay.

'I know that. They've already drummed it into us.'

'It could have been a lot worse, darling, he could have got hooked on drugs,' said Jim helpfully.

Peter nearly choked on his coffee. It was a couple of minutes before he recovered.

'I absolutely hate drugs,' he finally managed to say between more coughing fits.

'That's very good to hear, Peter,' said Kay.

'Have you told Mandy I'm not drinking any more?'

'Yes, she knows all about that. Hopefully we can report back positively again tonight. You understand I'll have to inspect the whole house from top to bottom a little later.'

He felt a moment of panic. He sincerely hoped she did not mean it literally. Still the crack was well hidden. He felt a bit hot though.

'Do you want that last bun, darling, or shall I have it?' asked Jim.

She picked up the plate crossly and thrust it under his nose.

'You're an absolute pig,' said Kay.

'Perhaps I should have bought more,' said Peter, anxious to avoid a rift.

Jim broke the bun in half with his fingers and put one half on his wife's plate.

'Where did you buy those buns, Peter? I must buy some myself,' said Kay.

Peter felt pleased with himself. He was well and truly back in her good books.

'How's the new job coming along?' asked Kay.

'Well, it keeps the wolf from the door. Hopefully I can get a better paid one soon.'

'You've sold your car, haven't you?' asked Jim.

'I just thought it was a bit extravagant at the moment.'

'Can I have a look round, please?' said Kay.

'Yes… yes, of course, I'll come with you. You won't need to go into the loft, will you?'

'No, Peter, I won't need to look in the loft.'

He had taken the vacuum cleaner out of mothballs that very day so he felt reasonably confident on that score. She peeked into every room but thankfully decided against taking up the carpet and excavating under the floorboards. They returned to the living room a few minutes later. Peter felt mightily relieved.

'Some of the rooms need air freshener but it's passable,' said Kay as she gathered up her handbag ready to leave. 'Louise is as good as gold at the moment, Peter. Mandy is coping very well,' she added.

'I always knew she'd make a wonderful mum,' said Peter.

'She wants to go back to work in a couple of months,' added Kay.

Peter went outside into the driveway to see them off. The cold clear night was a reminder that winter was well under way. He waved goodbye and watched them go. He walked towards the garage and lifted up the door. The ten-year-old blue Astra, which he had picked up for less than £1,000 with 98,000 miles on the clock, stood in the driveway. He drove it into the garage and locked the door. He hoped that the MOT due next month wouldn't be too costly.

Donna was in a filthy mood when he went to visit her the next day. He was shocked to find her trying to extract an extra five pounds from him before any sexual activity took place.

'My costs are going up and I need more money,' she whined at him as he removed his tie. 'Did you bring the condoms with you as I asked on the phone?'

Peter dutifully handed them over. He was starting to despair of this woman. *What sort of hooker*, he wondered, *couldn't provide condoms for her clients*. Besides, he found it demeaning having to bring his own.

'I was too fucking tired to go down town to buy some this morning,' she explained after he quizzed her about the oversight.

Peter removed his shirt.

'This flat is bloody freezing,' he protested. 'I'm not taking any more clothes off until you put the fire on.'

She reluctantly put on one bar of a small electric fire.

'Stop fucking complaining, I'll soon warm you up. Lie on your front so I can massage your back first. Do you want talc or oil?'

'Just get on with it, Donna.'

Her ice-cold hands made him wince and cry out. She warmed her hands in front of the fire, muttering to herself. He left a few minutes later, feeling discontented. His love affair with Donna had come to an end.

The January evenings were starting to draw out as Peter knocked on Mandy's door. Mandy opened the door, holding Louise wrapped in a pretty knitted shawl. She passed her to him and they went into the living room. Peter loved to hold his captivating daughter on his fortnightly visits to see Mandy and Louise. Soon, however, Louise started to cry.

'I think she's hungry,' said Mandy as Peter handed her back. 'I've got plenty of milk for her,' she said as Louise buried her mouth in her mother's breast, sucking vigorously.

'How are you getting on with your new job?' asked Mandy.

'Not too bad. The money is pretty poor but I haven't managed to find anything better. Are you still going back to work at the bank next month?'

'Yes, I want to. Mum has volunteered to look after Louise.'

'Yeah, it's probably a good idea for you to go back to work. Mothers shouldn't have to stay at home looking after their children unless they want to. You've got a good job as well.'

'I'm glad you agree. I certainly don't want to stay at home and not speak to anyone all day.'

'Look, Mandy, why don't you come back and live with me? We could try again.'

He saw her face tighten. She wouldn't look him in the face.

'I want to leave things as they are at the moment.'

'Do you want a divorce?'

'Probably, but let's not make a final decision yet. I want to be on my own.'

Peter felt distraught but could see she was adamant and would not budge. Kay had said to be patient but he knew it was crucifying him. He said goodbye, kissing Mandy on the cheek and holding Louise's tiny hand for a few precious seconds. This was always the most painful moment for him. He wondered if Mandy realised just how unbearable it was. He left with a sinking heart, longing for the next two long weeks to pass as quickly as possible.

150

Chapter Fifteen

It was a long time since Sue and her sister had been ice skating at the Plymouth Pavilions. They used to go together when the place first opened but since Sue had moved away to Torbay the activity had been dropped.

'I hope I can still remember how to stay upright,' said Sue as they waited in line to hire skates.

The impressive rink was moderately busy as Sue gingerly stepped onto the ice for the first time in three and a half years. It wasn't quite like the old days but she only fell over once.

'The pool is packed,' said Jo as they had a quick glance at the fun pool on leaving. They made their way to the refreshment area next to the entrance and sat down for coffee.

'Are you back in Tavistock permanently?' asked Jo.

'Let's wait and see. I've applied for three jobs in Plymouth so I'm keeping my fingers crossed. I've got a sore throat and a twitchy nose today so I may have caught a cold,' said Sue.

'Well, stay away from me if you have, I don't want to get it,' replied Jo.

Sue suffered a heavy cold but the rest of the family had not yet succumbed to the bug. The Lemsip remedy had possibly shortened her misery and now only a persistent cough and nasal congestion remained as a minor irritant. Still, she had no intention of rising from her warm bed until lunchtime. Finally she responded to her mother's dulcet tones urging her to get up and come down for lunch. She suddenly remembered the post, got out of bed and put on her dressing gown. It was about time she heard something about the jobs she had applied for.

Her parents had already started eating when she sat down at the table, yawning. Her father, she noticed sadly, had aged considerably since she had been away in London, his grey hair now turning white although he was only fifty-three.

'It's freezing outside. A really cold March wind,' said her mother.

'Have you got the day off today, Mum?' asked Sue.

'No, I'm working from three to eight. There's a letter for you.'

She grabbed it quickly as her father held it out to her. She ripped it open as quickly as she could and let out an excited cry as she skimmed through the first paragraph.

'I've got an interview for a job in Plymouth next Tuesday. This is the one I want.'

'You're very restless, Sue,' said her father.

'I've been home nearly a month, Dad. I don't want to sit on my backside for too long.'

'It's time you settled down, young lady,' said her father pointedly. Sue gave him a withering look.

'Just because I'm the oldest doesn't mean I have to get married first. In fact it's quite likely I may never get married. There's a lot to be said for living in sin.'

She saw a disapproving look appear on his face. 'That's not the way your grandparents brought me up.'

'Leave her alone, Jack, she's got her own life to lead,' said her mother.

'Tomorrow, Mum, I won't be here.'

'Where are you going?'

'To Paignton to see Sally and the new baby. I shouldn't be back too late. I'll leave here about nine thirty.'

'You haven't seen the baby yet, have you?'

'No, I haven't. It's a boy called Bradley. I'm looking forward to seeing them both.'

Sue lay in bed tossing and turning. She was thinking the unthinkable. Why couldn't she get him out of her mind? He had let her down badly but she had sought a terrible revenge. Now she felt guilty about what she had done. Tomorrow she would be returning to Torbay to see Sally but would it be so outrageous if she called on him just to see what state he was in. Mandy, despite the baby, wouldn't entertain the idea of returning to live with him. She found it impossible to sleep. She felt excited. She recalled the thrill she had felt whenever they had made love. She got up for a few minutes to make a hot drink but when she returned to bed she found that sleep still eluded her. Perhaps tomorrow would be the most important day of her life!

Sue felt nervous as she drove into the village of Collaton St Mary on the outskirts of Paignton, although it had only been four and a half months since she had left Torbay.

She pulled the car over to the side of the road, opposite the post office, and switched the radio on to calm her nerves. It felt strange coming back to the place which held so many bitter memories for her. She had sought refuge in London but that had failed and now she was back, if only for a day, where she started. She had not slept a wink until three in the morning and then she had woken again, two hours later, still wrestling with the same conundrum. An hour later she thought she had made a final decision. Now, sitting in the car biting her fingernails, she was not so sure.

Today she knew was a pivotal day in her life. She had made so many mistakes with men and now she was terrified of making another one. Sue knew she would have to make the decision on her own as she couldn't face talking to Sally about it. She switched the engine back on and prepared to drive the two miles to Sally's house but still she hadn't made up her mind.

'Shall we take Bradley down to Broadsands Beach after lunch and walk along the front?' suggested Sally.

'Let's do that, Sal. He seems to have got some wind, shall I hand him back to you?'

Sally took hold of him and gently patted him on the back. He was a large baby with almost no hair and cried a lot but to Sally, Sue could see, he was perfection.

Sally folded up the pushchair and carefully placed it in the boot. Bradley was safely strapped in the back seat by his proud father.

'It's a chilly wind; I hope he'll be warm enough. It could bucket down as well by the look of it,' said Bill. He waved them goodbye as Sally drove the mile to the beach.

'I'm going to park in the road like everyone else. Why should I pay car parking charges in the winter,' said Sally.

Sue started to giggle but her nerves were still jangling. She desperately wanted to confide in her friend but knew the ultimate decision was hers alone. What a trying eighteen months it had been. One disaster after another. Now, perhaps it was time for action. They only ventured a little way as the sky looked threatening. A few hardy souls joined them as they strolled along the promenade, past the café, the bracing wind, blowing in strongly from the sea.

'What about a new job?' enquired Sally.

'Well, that's in the lap of the gods but I've got an interview in Plymouth next week. Wish me luck.'

'Things didn't work out for you in London.'

'I wouldn't have missed the experience for the world but I had a slight problem with a man.'

'Really! You do surprise me. Was it the one who took you to Hawaii?' asked Sally.

'Yes, I found out he was two-timing me and he hit me. I ran a mile after that.'

'I don't know much about London. I've only been a couple of times. What was it like?'

'The job was okay and I saw a few West End shows but I never really felt at home in London. Islington was a strange sort of place but it had some good restaurants.'

'You amaze me, Sue. I would have thought London would have suited you down to the ground.'

'Not really. I would have stayed if things had worked out differently. I'm glad I'm back in Devon as long as I can get a decent job.'

They returned to the car just as the heavens opened and a heavy downpour ensued. On their return home Bradley exercised his vocal cords and had to be comforted by Sally. Eventually it was time for his afternoon nap and he fell asleep.

'We might have another one soon,' said Bill as they sat down for a cup of tea.

Sue grinned back in admiration. Soon however she became restive and at four thirty decided to leave.

'Why are you leaving so early?' asked Sally, looking disappointed.

'I promised to look in on another friend before I went home, Sal.'

Sue needed more time to think. She parked her car on Paignton seafront near the multiplex cinema, and looked at her watch. She would go round at six thirty unless of course, she changed her mind in the meantime. What had he been doing during the last few months? Perhaps he had met another woman.

She locked the car door and went for a walk along the front towards the pier. She stopped at a shelter and gazed out over the choppy sea. A few ships were already sheltering in Tor Bay as the wind, as forecast, started to pick up. Sue pulled her coat tighter round her neck as she made her way back towards the car. She looked at her watch again. Why was the big hand taking so long to move? She was definitely going to try and see him but she must wait until six thirty. At long last it was time to go; Sue knew it was now or never!

She parked her car in the road just a few yards from his house and looked at herself in the vanity mirror; her windswept hair badly needed some attention. Her mouth was as dry as a bone. A touch of red lipstick might be appropriate; she reached into her handbag and carefully applied it to her lips. Satisfied, she locked the car door and approached his front door with trepidation her hands sticky and trembling. She rang the bell. Almost immediately she heard the sound of footsteps. The door opened.

'Hello, Philip.'

For a moment he stood transfixed, unable to speak, and then he rushed towards her and she felt his hot breath on her face as he embraced her. It seemed to be ages before his vice-like grip eased her red lipstick now plastered all over his mouth and cheek.

'I was passing and I wanted to see how you all were.'

She felt the tears misting up her eyes. He took hold of her hand and pulled her inside.

'It's wonderful to see you, Sue. How are you?'

'I'm fine. I've come back to live in Devon – London's not for me. Philip, your face is all smudged, let me get a wet tissue and wipe it off.'

Matt and Clive appeared in the doorway, smiling. She resisted the cliché about how much they had grown, but it was true, they had. She gave them both a strong hug. They didn't seem to find this too unbearable.

By seven thirty it was almost like old times. Sue was in the kitchen planning to cook dinner and hoping Philip would give her a hand. Sue polished off a mug of hot tea, which she had been longing for almost the whole time since she had left Sally and Bill, and then carried out an inspection of the freezer.

'What were you planning to have for dinner, Philip?'

'I was going to do plaice, oven chips, peas, brown rolls and butter. Then the rest of the flan from yesterday.'

'All of it liberally sprinkled with tomato ketchup,' said Sue, grinning.

'No, don't worry they haven't started to put it on the flan yet,' said Philip, laughing.

Sue, whose appetite had been non-existent all day, now found it had been miraculously restored.

'The food sounds great – I fancy some of that myself.'

She pushed her face towards him and their lips briefly touched.

'I suppose I'd better phone home and say I won't be home tonight,' said Sue as they sipped their coffee in the living room after the meal. 'Have the boys gone upstairs?'

'They are watching football on satellite so we can talk in peace,' replied Philip.

'How are they now?'

'They are still missing their mother a lot but they are getting on well at school.'

'They're bound to miss their mother. You can't expect anything else.'

'Yes, I realise that but I'm finding it very difficult looking after them and running a business.'

'Do you still want me, even though I walked out on you?'

'Yes, I still want you. I've missed you terribly since you left. Come and live with us, Sue.'

She let out a nervous giggle. 'I might have to. Remember I burnt my boats when I gave up my flat. Look, Philip, I think I would like to see if it will work. Please be patient with me. The last eighteen months have been so difficult for me. Perhaps I've grown up in the last few months.'

'You can have your old job back.'

'That's sweet of you, Philip, but I've got an interview for a job in Plymouth on Tuesday and I want to go through with that. If I get the job I can travel to Plymouth in forty minutes. Please let me give you an answer later.'

She looked at him and saw him nod his approval.

Later they made love more urgently than they had ever done before. *Absence really does make the heart grow fonder*, she thought as his ardour pleasantly surprised her. She smiled to herself as she remembered how apprehensive she had been only a few hours before. Now it was as if they were carrying on exactly from where they had left off, almost six months ago. There was not a hint of resentment in his manner. Sue felt guilty, her decision to abandon them for the high life in London a nagging sore in her side. She wondered if she could make it up to them in the future but she was sure now she wanted to give it her best shot and try her best.

Sue was under no illusion that every evening with Clive and Matt would be harmonious. She felt mentally and physically exhausted after a sleepless twenty-four hours. A long sleep was required she needed at least eight hours. She had no intention at all of rising early on Sunday morning.

Tuesday turned out to be a red-letter day for Sue. Firstly, the job was in the bag apart from the formality of obtaining two references and Philip would be only too happy to provide one of those. Secondly, her car was bulging at the seams with all her gear. Heaven help her if the police saw that she couldn't see properly out of her rear window or any of the windows come to that. Suitcases in the boot and all the miscellaneous items, mostly clothes, jammed tight into every nook and cranny. It was certainly heavy going when travelling uphill.

Sue arrived just after the boys had returned from school. She conscripted their help in unloading and they didn't complain much until the job had almost been completed.

'Put those clothes on the bed, boys, and please be careful,' urged Sue, worried that her dresses might get damaged.

By six o'clock she felt confident enough to sit down on the settee and relax, feeling pleased with herself. This, she reckoned, was almost the point of no return – the day she moved most of her possessions into his house.

'I think I've got the job,' she announced excitedly as soon as Philip got inside the front door.

He gave her a hug as she joined him in the hall. 'Well done! Are they paying you a lot more than I did?'

She quickly did some calculations in her head.

'It probably works out about the same when you take in travelling costs, but that's not the point. This job is a real challenge.'

'Perhaps you can supplement your income by helping me sometimes,' said Philip.

'Of course I can, but you don't need to pay me.'

He smiled at her.

'You look pleased with yourself and that's an important consideration. How much of your stuff did you manage to get in the car?'

'Well over half. I've still got some clothes to bring. We might need to buy one or two wardrobes, there's quite a lot of things upstairs.'

She gasped as she saw the time.

'The boys will be starving!'

She set to work with gusto, her mood more relaxed than she could remember for a very long time.

Later, in bed, she confided in Philip.

'When I came to see you last Saturday I was very nervous. I don't know why. I wanted to write to you when I was in London but there never seemed to be any spare time. Did you think I might come back?'

'No, I thought you were gone for ever.'

He wiped his eyes with the back of his hand. She handed him a tissue and he blew hard on it.

'I don't just want you so that you can help me look after Matt and Clive, you know. I love you.'

Sue reached into the box for another tissue and she blew hard on it. As she snuggled up close to Philip, feeling safe and wanted Sue thought fleetingly of a more exciting lover. Perhaps he had caught her on the rebound but she knew one thing for certain – Philip was one of the best people she had ever met.

Chapter Sixteen

Peter was sorry it had come to this but he reckoned he had no alternative if he wanted to keep the house. He had made a concerted effort to give up the crack cocaine but it had proved impossible. The withdrawal symptoms had frightened him, made him depressed and his craving had increased. Soon he had relapsed and now he was taking more crack than ever. He struggled in vain to see a way out of his predicament as his financial position had, once again, become critical. It was time for drastic action!

He walked into his father's rundown taxi office and pleaded for assistance.

'I thought you got a good deal when you sold the Escort.'

'Yeah, I did but I owed somebody a lot of money and I had to pay off a loan.'

'I thought you got a redundancy payment after you lost your job.'

'I did but I've still got fifty thousand on the mortgage. That's crippling me, Dad.'

His father shook his head sadly but pulled a set of keys out of his trouser pocket. He proceeded to open a locked drawer in a cabinet and pulled out a wad of notes. He counted for a few seconds and handed some over.

'There's two hundred to help you out, that's all I can afford at the moment. Business has been very bad lately and I'm not sure how much longer I can keep going. I laid one driver off last week.'

'Thanks, dad, you're a lifesaver. I'm sure I'll be able to pay you back soon.'

'You need your wife back. I always liked Mandy – lovely girl.'

'I want her back as well, you know. She had depression but she's snapped out of it now.'

'I haven't seen my granddaughter yet.'

Peter felt the guilt inside him increase.

'I promise I'll make sure you see Louise soon, Dad.'

His father's ageing lined face broke into a weak smile. 'That would be nice, Peter. That would be very nice.'

Peter stepped out of the shabby office into the late spring sunshine. The brightness made him shield his eyes with his hand as he walked quickly to his car. He felt disillusioned. Two hundred measly pounds. What use was that to a man in his position? Was he all washed up at the ridiculously early age of thirty-one? He had not given up hope entirely though. He would be seeing his mother in Totnes in a few hours. He sincerely hoped she could do a lot better than his father. He knew only too well that this was virtually his last chance.

His mother and aunt looked well and were soon badgering him with questions about Louise and Mandy. He was anxious to broach the subject of money at the first available opportunity but that was impossible while his aunt remained in the room, plying him with questions.

'I can't understand why Mandy ever left you. Doesn't she realise what a responsible boy you've always been?'

Peter cringed with embarrassment and felt himself blushing. He saw the two women look at each other obviously in total agreement.

'Did you bring the photographs with you, dear?'

Peter reached inside his sports jacket and handed them over.

'I took them last week. They've come out very well.'

'It's hard to believe she's over six months old. Look, June, she's holding herself up in this one,' said his mother, gleefully.

'I see Mandy took some of them. This one's very good of you and Louise,' said his aunt.

Eventually, to Peter's great relief, his aunt left the room to prepare a meal. Peter felt bad again but he decided that if he ventured nothing he would gain nothing. He plunged in, hoping for the best!

'Mum, I've run into a few financial difficulties. Can you help me out please?' He saw a look of concern on her face.

'What sort of difficulties?'

'I owe a lot on my credit card and then there's the large mortgage and I have to give Mandy some money for Louise.'

'Have you asked your father?'

'He's almost skint, Mum. The taxi business is struggling.'

'Serves him right for messing up our life.'

Peter shut his eyes and looked away. He hated to see her so bitter.

'I thought you had a full-time job now.'

'I do have a full-time job but it's not well paid. This has been building up for some time.'

His mother went quiet. He glanced over at her and he could see she was assessing the situation. After a minute she stood up and, without a word, left the room. Peter felt hopeful but didn't want to get carried away. A few moments later she returned armed with a chequebook.

'This thousand pounds is yours. You don't have to pay it back. It's to help you straighten your life out. You don't look well to me, Peter.'

He crossed the room took the cheque and planted a kiss firmly on her cheek.

'I'm sixty-two years old, Peter. I'm going to need the rest of my money for my old age.'

'Thanks, Mum, you've saved my life.' He suspected it was only a stay of execution but at least he had a lifeline to hang on to. He stayed for the meal his aunt had prepared but now that he had got what he wanted he was anxious not to be home late.

'I haven't been over to your house for ages, Peter, I wish I had learnt to drive,' said his mother as she saw him off at the doorstep.

His craving for the crack cocaine hit him almost as soon as he got inside the front door. He wanted so much to conquer his addiction to the white powder that was destroying his existence and live a normal life again. He knew he badly needed help. A daring thought came into mind. What would be the reaction of the one person who could possibly help him if he told her the unpalatable truth? He agonised about the wisdom of telling her as he knew she hated drugs. Was it worth the risk? In these circumstances, with his life in a total vicious downward spiral, what had he got to lose?

As usual, as regular as clockwork, he was round to see Mandy and Louise the following week. Mandy's mother, unsmiling and uncompromising, opened the front door for Peter. Mandy was watching Louise crawl across the floor as he entered the lounge. He walked over to the other side of the room, scooped his daughter up in his arms, and kissed her before putting her down on the floor again. He thought of kissing Mandy but decided against it.

'Did they like the photos?' she asked.

'Not half! They were thrilled with them.'

'Tell your mum I'll bring Louise over to see them again soon.'

'My dad's only seen photos of her. Can he come with me next time?'

'Of course, bring him along. That's a great idea. I like your dad.'

Louise started to cry and Mandy went to see what was wrong.

'She needs changing. Excuse me a minute, I won't be long.'

Peter felt a nervous wreck while she was out of the room. He pondered the situation before she returned. Knowing how she detested all drugs, she could throw him out of the house and he might never see either of them again. On the other hand she might understand and want to help him. Where was Mandy? Surely it didn't take this long to change Louise.

Mandy returned with a clean baby and handed Louise to Peter. He sat down with Louise on his lap and she looked as though she might fall asleep. He reasoned that Mandy was less likely to hit him over the head with a chair if he was holding Louise. Mandy started fidgeting with some baby clothes.

'Mandy, can you come and sit down a moment, please?'

She came and sat down on the easy chair close to him.

'I don't know how to tell you this but I'm in terrible trouble. I don't know how it… I don't know what to do.'

He felt the tears streaming down his face and he reached inside his trouser pocket for his handkerchief and wiped his eyes. Mandy moved over and sat perched on the end of the settee next to him.

'What on earth is the matter, Peter?'

'Well… well, you know I've got on top of the drink problem. I haven't touched a drop in months.'

'Yes, you've done very well but you shouldn't have started in the first place.'

'Yeah, I realise that, Mandy, but I've got a bigger problem to deal with now. I don't know how to tell you.'

'Are you ill?' She looked petrified.

'No… no, Mandy, I'm not ill. Well, maybe in one sense I am. I can't cope with it any more.'

'What are you talking about? What is it?'

'Drugs!' He closed his eyes to avoid the look of horror on her face.

'What drugs, Peter? Tell me which drugs you've been taking?' she bellowed at him.

'It started with cannabis but now it's crack. I thought I could stop but now I find I can't. It's awful!'

He braced himself as he could see she was distraught.

'You stupid fool, Peter, after all I've said to you about how I hate drugs.'

He pulled out his handkerchief again and wiped his eyes. He couldn't stop the tears. He finally looked at her and saw that she was shocked rigid by his confession, unable to speak.

'I was… under a lot of pressure. It just seemed… it just seemed to happen. Please come back to me and help me sort myself out. I want you both back home with me.'

'I don't know, Peter. You let me down badly. Now I find you've let me down again.'

He felt his control snap. 'I wouldn't be in this mess if you hadn't left me. It's all your fault!'

He saw the anger on her face.

'Don't blame me, Peter! You betrayed me just like your father betrayed your mother! I loved you!'

She rushed to the door in tears and he could hear her running up the stairs. He decided not to follow her. He glanced down at his beautiful daughter and saw that, despite the mayhem, she was fast asleep, seemingly without a care in the world. He gave her a little kiss on her soft skin and protectively put her back in the cot. Mandy's mother poked her head round the door, an angry look on her face.

'Mandy's crying her eyes out Peter. What on earth have you done to upset her this time?'

'Mind your own business, it's between Mandy and me.'

He took a final look at Louise and then walked to the front door. Mandy's mum was holding the door open for him. He didn't bother to say goodbye.

Peter was sorely tempted to call in at the first available pub on his way home but somehow his nerve held. He knew he was in a mountain of trouble as it was and now he had just made it worse. Luckily he still had the crack at home and that would have to do. Once he got a quick snort up his nose his troubles would evaporate. He did not consider how he would feel the next morning, that was an eternity away.

Peter sat in pitch-black darkness feeling sorry for himself and the worse for wear. It had been a calamitous mistake to tell Mandy the truth and now, predictably, she was seething with anger. Hopefully after three days, she would have calmed down a bit. He hoped his impetuosity had not endangered his fortnightly visits. He felt so depressed about the whole insoluble nightmare. He couldn't bear it if she tried, urged on by her mother, to stop him seeing Louise. Suddenly the sound of the telephone ringing caught his attention. He swore under his breath but decided to answer it before the answering machine cut in. He was surprised to hear a familiar voice. It was Mandy!

'How are you, Peter?'

'I'm feeling a bit down at the moment. I've been sitting here in the dark, thinking.'

'About what?'

'I think you can probably guess. I didn't mean to upset you the other night, you know.'

'I know you didn't and I'm glad you told me. Peter, you've got yourself in a terrible mess.'

'Don't worry, I'll be okay, Mandy. Can I still come over with Dad next time?'

'You won't be okay on your own. I can see you won't so I'm coming back.'

Peter could hardly believe what he was hearing. He felt euphoric, his vanishing hopes suddenly rekindled.

'That's great, Mandy! That's wonderful!'

'I'm only coming back if you're prepared to help yourself. I've got Louise to think about.'

'I want to stop, Mandy. I want to stop but I can't.'

'Perhaps Louise and I can help you if we come back, but you've got to help yourself as well.'

'Well, I gave up the drink. When are you coming?'

'Tomorrow if you want. I need you to come over and collect some of my things. My parents won't help, they say I'm bonkers going back to you.'

'Never mind them. What time do you want me to come over?'

'Six would be a good time. We need to think about Louise. I hope that's a good time for you.'

'Yeah, that's fine. I'll come straight from work. See you tomorrow.'

Peter jumped for joy. This was totally unexpected and now he had to set to work making the house as welcoming as possible. He worked his fingers to the bone as he washed all the dishes and vacuumed the carpets. He sat down, feeling tired but elated. But by ten he started to feel the usual symptoms and his craving started to get the upper hand. He badly needed a snort and decided his rehabilitation could wait a little longer. Mandy would understand that Rome wasn't built in a day, as she always did. He reached deep inside the kitchen cupboard and pulled out the precious white packet. He only needed a quick one and he would be fine.

Mandy had only been back two days and, to Peter's chagrin, she was already laying down the law.

'You must go and see your doctor as soon as possible. I expect you'll have to attend a drug clinic as well.'

'Do I have to? Perhaps I can do it on my own.'

'No, you can't. You were horrible last night when you needed a fix. You must do as I say or I'm leaving you again. Do you understand?'

Peter felt wretched partly because he still hadn't told the whole truth. Was this a good time to tell her? He plucked up his courage again.

'Mandy, there's something else I need to tell you.'

She sighed and a worried expression appeared on her face. 'What is it now, Peter?'

'I owe a lot of money. I'm over my limit on my credit card and I'm one month behind with the mortgage repayments.'

'How much do you owe on the credit card?'

'Three grand. The interest rate is nearly twenty per cent.'

He saw her assessing the problem and was pleased to see that she appeared to be taking the whole matter in her stride.

'We can use some of my grandmother's money to clear that. It's only sitting in the building society earning interest at the moment and I can draw out the money immediately. The same goes for the mortgage.'

'That would be a great help, Mandy. I've been getting in deeper and deeper recently.'

She turned her attention to other things.

'Look at the state of this carpet, Peter. It badly needs a shampoo. They look like drink stains to me.'

He had to confess that she was probably right and she turned quickly away in disgust. He followed her into the utility room as she went in search of carpet shampoo.

'Right, Peter, I've found the shampoo. You can make yourself useful by getting a bucket of hot water. We've got an applicator so let's do the whole carpet.'

Peter started running the water.

'You won't tell Kay and Jim about the crack, will you?'

'No, I won't. At least not as long as you're prepared to help yourself.'

'She'll kill me if she finds out.'

'So will I if you let me down again. Remember you've got two of us to look after. If you want Louise and I to stay with you you've got to get yourself right. I'm going to help you as much as I can. At least you've got a job.'

Peter let out a loud laugh. 'I only clear about £200 a week – you earn more than me.'

'That's not important, Peter.'

'It is to me. I want to get a better job.'

He heard Louise crying upstairs.

'You start on the carpet and I'll see to Louise,' said Peter. He rushed upstairs to find her sopping wet. He thought of calling to Mandy for assistance but stopped in his tracks. Why did he need Mandy? He had never changed a nappy in his life but now seemed as good a time as any to learn how.

Peter returned to the living room, holding Louise.

'I've changed her, she was all wet.'

Mandy dropped the applicator and came to investigate. Peter waited with bated breath for her verdict. She gave him a smile.

'Very good, Peter – you must do that more often. Please put her back in the cot and come and help me.'

He returned a minute or so later and started brushing as Mandy took a rest.

'Oh, I forgot to tell you, Jim and Kay want to take us out for a drink on Saturday. You can have a non-alcoholic drink. Louise can stay with Mum and Dad so I said yes.'

Peter felt pleased it would be nice for all four of them to go out together again. He couldn't recall the last time it had happened but it must have been almost two years. He turned his mind back to the job in hand and saw that the stains had gone and the rust-coloured carpet looked almost as good as new.

Kay had a new shorter hairstyle and her mousy-coloured hair looked attractive. Mandy complemented her on the new look as they entered The Rose and Crown.

'I've been at the hairdresser's most of the afternoon and he suggested I have it cut shorter,' said Kay.

Jim went to the bar to order drinks and Peter followed him to help carry them back to their table.

'Peter, we both want ice,' he heard Kay shout above the din.

'This place is always packed on a Saturday,' said Jim as he handed over a ten-pound note to the barmaid.

The incessant loud music made it difficult to talk without shouting. Peter was content with his non-alcoholic beverage and a packet of nuts. He handed them round to the others. Kay had a smirk on her face and he couldn't make out why. Eventually she let him in on the secret.

'Peter, you know the significance of us having a drink in this particular pub, don't you?' said Kay grinning from ear to ear.

Peter was nonplussed. He looked across at Mandy who was smiling broadly.

'I'm disappointed you don't remember,' said Mandy, laughing.

Peter wracked his brain but couldn't come up with any answers.

'She remembers even if you don't,' said Kay infuriatingly.

Peter turned to Jim for help but unfortunately he had a blank look on his face.

'All I know is the ladies insisted on coming to this pub,' said Jim.

Kay put them out of their misery. 'You men are hopeless. This is where the four of us spent the evening together on the day that the two of you met for the first time,' said Kay, looking straight at Peter. 'There have been times during the last two and a half years when I've had reason to doubt my sanity for being the instigator that brought the two of you together. I hope my patience and fortitude have now been rewarded.'

Jim indulged in some mild hand clapping. Peter felt pleased but a little embarrassed and took a long drink. Jim raised his glass.

'To Mandy and Peter.'

'Wrong, darling. To Mandy, Peter and Louise. Remember they're one item now – for the first time,' Kay said pointedly.

'As usual, you are right, Kay.'

He tried again. 'To Mandy, Peter and Louise – a happy future to the three of you.'

The four of them touched glasses. Peter sat back, momentarily free from worry and guilt and a wry grin passed his lips. He feared Kay would skin him alive if she stumbled on the truth. He calculated it would be worth a lot of pain to avoid her wrath!

The others were talking animatedly together and Peter let his mind wander. He thought of Mandy and Louise and he looked across at Mandy, the beautiful girl he adored. Why, he asked himself, had he made his own life hell? He knew he now had one final opportunity to repair the damage he had caused and that he had only scratched the surface in his bid to overcome his addiction. Would it be enough to have the two people he loved more than anything in the world beside him to help him win his battle? He hoped they would give him the inspiration and willpower to succeed. Only time would tell.